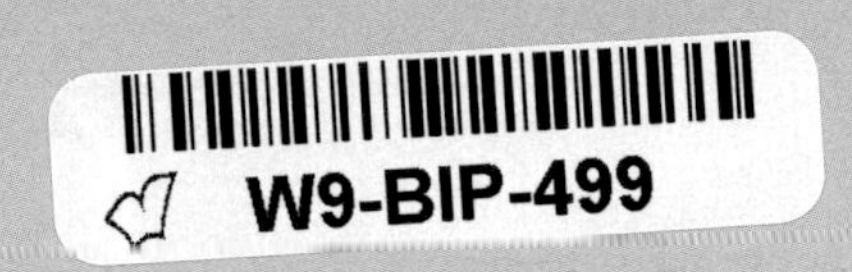

THE CONTEMPORARY
ART OF THE NOVELLA

THE CONTEMPORARY ART OF THE NOVELLA

LUCINELLA

LUCINELLA

LORE SEGAL

MELVILLEHOUSE
BROOKLYN, NEW YORK

LUCINELLA

FIRST PUBLISHED BY FARRAR, STRAUS AND GIROUX, 1976

FIRST MELVILLE HOUSE PRINTING: AUGUST 2009

MELVILLE HOUSE PUBLISHING
145 PLYMOUTH STREET
BROOKLYN, NY 11201

WWW.MHPBOOKS.COM

ISBN: 978-1-933633-79-4

BOOK DESIGN: KELLY BLAIR, BASED ON A SERIES DESIGN
BY DAVID KONOPKA

PRINTED IN CANADA.

LIBRARY OF CONGRESS CATALOGING-IN-PUBLICATION
DATA

SEGAL, LORE GROSZMANN.
LUCINELLA / LORE SEGAL.
P. CM.
ISBN 978-1-933633-79-4
1. WOMEN POETS—FICTION. 2. JEWS—NEW YORK
(STATE)—NEW YORK—FICTION. I. TITLE.
PS3569.E425L83 2009
813'.54—DC22
2009016783

Still and again
David

LUCINELLA

Lucinella Apologizes to the World for Using It

"What's the matter, Maurie?"

Maurie says a week ago he slept with a poet who kept her sharpened pencil underneath the pillow. At breakfast she stuck it behind her ear. Today she sent him the poem.

(He can't mean me, I know. I've never slept with Maurie and keep my pencil in my pocket at all times.)

"Isn't that a shabby thing to do by a friend?" he asks.

"But, Maurie, what's a poor poet to do with her excitements? Take them back to bed? Paste them in her album? Eat them? When all she wants is to be writing!"

"About the literary scene again!" says Maurie.

I ask him if he recognized himself.

"No," he says. "The man in the poem must be three other lovers."

"Did you recognize her?"

"Only the left rib out of which she'd fashioned a whole new woman."

"Will you publish it in *The Magazine?*"

"Yes," he says. "It's a good poem. But why won't the girl invent?"

"And don't you think she would, if she knew how? Pity her, Maurie. She'd prefer to write about sorcerers, ghosts, gods, heroes, but all she knows is you."

In the middle of the night I wake and know Maurie meant me. I call him on the telephone and say, "I use you too, and I know that is indefensible in friendship and as art."

Maurie waits for me to say, "And I'll never do it again," but I am silent a night and a day. For one month I cannot write a word. The following Monday I sit down, sharpen my pencil, and invent a story about Maurie and me having this conversation, which has taken root in a corner of my mind where it will henceforward sprout a small but perennial despair.

I put the story in an envelope and send it to Maurie.

Lucinella

1

Lucinella is my name. I wear glasses. It's my first visit here and I'm in love with all five poets, four men, one woman, and an obese dog called Winifred.

Winterneet's doctor has ordered exercise—yes, imagine! J. D. Winterneet is one of my fellow guests! He and I have fallen into the habit of walking round the lake, in the first white light before breakfast. I like Winterneet tremendously. He's older than the rest of us. We are people who write poetry, but Winterneet is a famous poet. His fame is very attractive. His head is bald and noble; everything below seems mere appendage. His feet, I'm sure, are baby pink. I keep thinking he will discover that half the time I don't know the half of what I'm saying. I tell him this, but Winterneet turns out to be a mensh. I think he just said he's read my poems, but a cloud stooped over my faculties and the moment is gone forever. No, it's not! Winterneet is saying what he enjoys is the way I squeeze the last drop out of my meaning before

I disintegrate it. I don't particularly recognize myself in this, but it sounds good. He says sometimes I'm very witty. In my chest, where I'm expecting pleasure, there's a hollow. I tell Winterneet this. He says, yes, praise never yields the promised pleasure, though every slight gives a full measure of pain, and being ignored is insupportable.

"Even you!" I say.

"Are you kidding!" he says.

He tells me stories about all the poets who've stayed here, at Yaddo. This Winterneet walking beside me has walked beside Roethke, breakfasted with Snodgrass and Jarrell—with Auden! Frost is his second cousin; he went to school with Pound, traveled all the way to Ireland once, to have tea with Yeats, and spent the weekend with the Matthew Arnolds. He remembers the time Keats threw up on his way home from anatomy; Winterneet says he admires Wordsworth's poetry, but couldn't stand the man. He loved Johnson and he won't read Boswell's final volume. He knew Stella well, he says, and hints *he* knows if she slept with the Dean or not.

He likes to hear my stories too and makes a space in his attention in which I blossom. He stands still and, turning to me with exactly the right tone of astonishment, says, "You *are* bright!" I'm pleased, and disappointed he didn't say I'm beautiful. I tell Winterneet my theory that we live on a seesaw between arrogance and abjection. His understanding what I mean turns me on.

I'm rubbing the spot one and one fourth of an inch above Winifred's tail, which makes him stretch his neck and, with his eyes closed, move his head infinitesimally side to side; the rest of us do not have our spots so handy.

Because Winifred is a real dog I have changed his sex to protect his privacy. The poets, Meyers, Winterneet,

Betterwheatling, Pavlovenka, and Bert, and more as needed, I will make up from scratch. No, that's not true. My invention needs a body to get it going, but I will set my own head on it. I will make up an eye here, borrow a nose or two there, and a mustache and something funny someone said and a pea-green sweater, so it's no use your fitting your keys into my keyholes, to try and figure out who's who.

I myself am a younger poet, twentyish going on forty. You haven't heard of me as yet. (Lucinella is the name.) In town I tend to be the introverted, intellectual type, but here I'm turning into a Russian novel. "I'm in love with all of you," I tell the poets. Poets understand this, and go on eating their breakfasts.

On my left, that's Meyers, putting brown sugar on his porridge. (You've read his latest, which won the Pulitzer five years ago—all about his fear that he is going crazy.) Across from us sits Betterwheatling, the English critic. (You see his name a lot in *The New York Review of Books*.) He's pouring coffee into Pavlovenka's teacup. Pavlovenka giggles. (You haven't heard of her, and probably won't.) She's forty, five foot by four by four, and a genuine Russian. Her passionate and happy eyes embrace us all. I can't take too much of Pavlovenka, but I do like her, and I really like Betterwheatling. (That's the English critic. Try to tell my poets apart, I know how hard it is.) Betterwheatling's wit is oblique and his dimensions are commodious (I like bulk), and I like his being English. Meyers I love. His face is white, his blue eyes are rimmed with pink, his great blond mustache droops. Meyers tells wonderful, funny stories. Also I like his Pulitzer.

I'm telling him my problem. Take this great, dark-paneled, sun-filled dining room, I say, in which we sit on nineteenth-century English chairs carved in imitation of medieval settles, with mild-faced, short-waisted warriors in high relief, poking their spears and sabers into our backs; or this great silver bowl full of roses in the center of the table: even when we don't focus on our physical surroundings they seep into our awareness. How can they seep into my poem, and without sneaking? I abhor tricks.

Because I know this has no relevance to Meyers's writing, I ask what he is working on. He says on a longer line with alternate end stops that's got him tied in knots.

He says, "Didn't Roethke use to come to Yaddo?"

Winterneet tells us about the time he drove Roethke up from the sanatorium. On the way, he says, Roethke spoke only once, to ask who else was staying. People frightened him, but it was late in the season—just about this time of year. The summer crowd had gone; it was a small, quiet bunch. Winterneet says he recalls the morning he and Roethke were walking behind the vegetable gardens and discovered the root cellar. (*Root cellar*. I'm going to write a poem called "Euphoria in the Root Cellar," all about some poets who visit a root cellar in a Roethke poem.)

"What *is* a root cellar?" I ask Meyers. Meyers is staring at Winterneet, who's saying, "Roethke used to work well at Yaddo, but some have come up and promptly gone to pieces."

"Who? What happened?" I ask. I love stories. But J. D. Winterneet has finished breakfast. He says he'll tell me on our walk tomorrow morning. He leaves.

Bert, the red-haired poet from New Jersey (no, I never heard of him either before this), comes late to breakfast and says moodily, "Morning all." I never quite believe in red-haired men, but Bert I like. We've been having lunch together, at noon, on the terrace.

Day after day the weather has been spectacular. The contour of every nearest leaf and farthest range of mountain is equally sharp. Winifred sinks his teeth into a mole's skull and shakes. The crisp snap of vertebra carries clear across the lake. The stone bench is hot to the touch; an old-fashioned scent of late roses weighs upon the air like the sentimental Virtues that willed this Property to the pursuit of Art.

In the poem I am going to write, my protagonist, made out of a left rib of Lucinella's, will walk in the rose garden looking for someone to be with and meet Pavlovenka (she's better than nobody). Pavlovenka will say come and look what she has found, she's not telling what! Lucinella will follow her past the vegetable garden, round the greenhouses, through the tall grass by the woodpile where there's a red roof set like a circumflex into the earth. At the other end it's higher and accommodates a door. Lucinella and Pavlovenka remove the soft, warmly, damply moldering detritus of half a dozen autumns and draw the door outward, bend down together, and stick their heads inside Poetry. Light filters through the purple dust turning the earth rose. Look! Shards from a figured urn, and there, in that corner, glows an enormous, ruined spiderweb made of such filament as Rumpelstiltskin spun to sneak the miller's daughter into the king's bed and have a royal baby fathered upon her for himself, poor evil, wizened, hunchbacked Rumpelstiltskin! In my poem the two women gasp and exclaim and take each other by the hand.

Those neat figures moving round the fountain at the bottom of the great lawn are from the village. They look up. They never point. They're saying, "Up there, on the terrace in the sun—one of the poets!" But really it's only me! Or maybe they haven't noticed me. Nobody sees me. I'll run and write my poem, I'll sign it Lucinella. A magazine will publish it, the magazine will lie on the newsstand. You will pick it up, and read me, and the hollow in my chest will be filled up.

Now Bert leans out of the round turret where he has his study. He sees me and waves. Here he comes across the terrace, carrying a thermos and his lunch box, like a small black sarcophagus.

"What's up?" I say.

"Need you ask," says he. Bert and I have fallen hopelessly into obscenities with one another. It isn't clear yet what we intend. The full moon, which turns me back into a virgin, reseals for him the mystery of how to get a woman from the joke on the terrace, up two flights of stairs, and into bed. It makes him moody. "Hot," he says.

"Take it off," I say.

"Unilaterally?" says he.

"Go ahead then and be unilaterally cross."

His fleshy, brutal shoulders hulk inside a turquoise sweatshirt trimmed with white and orange braid. How did *he* fall into poetry, I ask him. He says it's a dull story. I say there *are* no dull stories. Glowering, Bert recalls how he discovered Milton in the Public Library at fifteen. He says he looked around at the librarian fishing a tissue out of her patent-leather pocketbook; at the girl taking notes from *Consumers' Research*. The ubiquitous old man who naps in libraries napped on. Bert wondered: This Milton has been around three hundred years and nobody knows it except me! Truth turns me on, and Bert's is not the New York kind that slides too easily from too much practice. He doesn't have the habit of autobiography, and steps awkwardly from one to another of the modest events that brought him from there to here. The revelation at boot camp, where that boy, who was later killed, wrote poems all about himself—not very good poems. With the GI Bill, Bert came to New York. His wife got a job at Macy's. He took a class with Lowell.

Once Lowell said to him, "That's just what *I'm* trying to do." Lowell got him translating. "Rilke," Bert says. His blunt orange profile broods over the parapet. He has forgotten me.

"Sometime," I say, "let me see some of your stuff." Why am I *asking* to see it? What will I do if he is terrible, which is statistically much more probable than that he's any good? Or if he's marvelous, what will I say then? "You don't want to see it," Bert says. He's upset. Like our old friend, the drowning man whose life is run backward at a speed that turns every voice into Donald Duck, Bert is reviewing his poems through my eyes, which are about to see his heart, his liver, and his lights, and that probably pompous couplet about the Bomb, which he should take out, except it might be the finest two lines he has ever written, and there's the poem he did yesterday, about the time he loosened his shoe and untied ecstasy between the loop and the knot; maybe I will be so good as to see an irony he didn't intend, and will I hear the howling vowels of the spectacular conclusion? In two seconds Bert's stomach lurches from arrogance to abjection, and ascends to fall and ascend again. He can't leave the manuscript for me on the table where we collect our mail and tack the little folded notes asking each other to tennis at four or drinks at 5:15. He doesn't trust the pages to lie still and contain him. How is he to achieve the unspeakably indelicate transfer of his work into my hands? He'll bring it around, he says, to my room, when I go up to change for dinner. "And slip it to me," I relentlessly, helplessly say.

One after another we find we're done with breakfast and fade out of the dining room. (Pavlovenka stays to keep Bert company, which will drive him up the wall.) We congregate again in the back rooms, where they have put out *The New York Times*. Winterneet's got the book section. I review the week's crises calmly: there's no explosion that can cross two hundred miles of upstate New York. I'm turning Republican!

Even after we have picked our lunch boxes off the shelf, we linger, reluctant to commit ourselves, till Winterneet slams down the *Times* and goes upstairs.

My study is some way along the drive. Betterwheatling's is further into the woods. We saunter in desultory talk, our minds already half on our work, where we do not entertain one another.

I sharpen my pencil and sit looking out the window. Pavlovenka walks by on her way to the woods. She likes to write her poems in the out-of-doors.

Pavlovenka's gone. A car drives by on muted tires and leaves the scene empty. Trees sparkle in the morning sun. Later two of the gardeners will pass with their equipment. Even Winifred, who has been brainwashed to believe poetry matters and poets should be cherished, goes about his business on silent paws. The staid, middle-aged housemaid in white linen looks in my door, sees me at my desk, and withdraws, but she can come in. I need to walk awhile.

A distant lawnmower hums like a summer insect; the smell of cut green grass makes my breasts sprout; the five live poets wrapped in cigarette paper and inhaled with the admixture of the breath of wild thyme which grows in patches on the great sloping lawn fill my lungs with euphoria. What I need is to be with someone.

I look into the mailroom. Meyers is sitting in the wicker armchair. "Did you see Max Peters's brutal review of Winterneet's new poems in the *Times Book Review?* It must be Sunday," he says. "Tomorrow I go home, and they'll fold all this away." He says he cannot bear it, and neither can I. We confess to each other that we can't bear to be parted for a minute and come to a decision: We won't work today!

Meyers and I, who write day in day out, seven mornings every week, and have for years and will for as long as we can think ahead, are going to play hooky together this sunny September Sunday. Guilty elation makes us lightheaded; we giggle over the *Times* crossword. Later we walk into the village, lean our heads over the dusty glass case in the local museum to see the doll's pewter tea set; a lot of fans; here's a pair of real Chinese shoes, impossibly small, that once bound the feet of a real Chinese lady; and a letter Teddy Roosevelt wrote in 1906 to the local actor who made good. Hilariously we burst back into sunlight.

The rest of the afternoon we sit in the bar and drink beer. "Did you see Winterneet acting like an infant who's lost a game of dominoes?" I say. "Winterneet on the wane," says Meyers. Not out of malice but from desire for communion, we chew up the other poets and offer them to one another. Meyers watches the ball game over my head. I eat peanuts. We tell each other things. Yesterday, he says, he changed a comma to a period-capital-A and copied the whole poem over and saw it should have been a comma, changed it back, and copied it over, and changed it back to a period. All day, for a week, for months, he has been changing this same comma and can't go on until he gets it right. Meyers touches trembling fingers to his drooping blond mustache. I keep eating peanuts.

Logy with beer, our eyes tending to close on us, we totter back to dinner.

In my poem Pavlovenka will giggle: "Everybody guess what we found in the garden!" After dinner, if they're good, she says, we'll show them. Betterwheatling will pick up Pavlovenka's poor word "good" and play her like a ball on his fountain of words, not unkindly, but briefly. Tiring of her simplicity he'll turn to ask Winterneet about his publisher, and Pavlovenka, glowing from the exhilaration of being teased, will fall to the ground and say very loudly, "After dinner, everybody! Meet outside the back door. Lucinella and I will show you we're not telling what!"

After dinner we move into the drawing room. From the great plate window, which gives onto the terrace, which overlooks the lawn, three orange Paisley carpets, placed end to end, reach to the far side of the drawing room, where a marble fountain tinkles day and night. In this Peaceable Kingdom we six poets sit on pink velvet couches under the full-length portrait of our Edwardian patroness, who, without hint of self-consciousness or irony, had herself framed in a half ton of gold leaf. Our inappropriateness, one to another, with respect to age, fame, and excellence, charms me, and I look with an equal fondness at Winterneet in his neat shoes and banker's blue, like a minus quantity; at Bert's hick suit of iridescent and too-light gray; at Betterwheatling wearing his trousers like an English duke of a Sunday morning, baggy and antique; at Meyers's mod and faggy tights, the kind tapestry courtiers wear to hunt the unicorn, outlining his handsome sex, and it seems sweet to me, and friendly, how each carries his, some more useful than others but each appropriate to himself; and Pavlovenka in her red-and-white-striped socks, her skirts above her monumental polished knees, like twin worlds; and me, trying for chic.

In the music room someone's put Bach on the phonograph, which, with the superfluity of beer inside me, explains this tendency to tearfulness. It's not playing fair, it isn't done, it isn't classical to reach around the outside of the music into one's heart. (*That's* what I want to do in my poem.) I say, "Good night. I have to go and write a line or two so I can go to bed."

Here's Betterwheatling, in the scented darkness. He says, "Walk me round the lake before I go and do another page or two of my beastly book." Some large, feathered thing panics and flaps in the bushes. Betterwheatling turns to it and says, "Go to sleep." The trees are dense over our heads and shut out the paler black of the sky. "Where are you, Betterwheatling?" I ask him. Betterwheatling, who's invented himself to fit himself, wears himself like an old slipper. What's he hiding? "What are you hiding, Betterwheatling?" I ask him if he saw J. D. Winterneet behaving like an infant who's lost a game of dominoes. But Betterwheatling mildly declines to join in my treachery. "It was a silly review," he says. And he refuses to be wise or tragical. "But, Betterwheatling," I say, "*you* know we're set to blow ourselves to pieces. Mankind reeks to heaven!" "We're noisy too," he says. I say even he and I keep our heels on the necks of the oppressed and he agrees. He says he loathes bad manners. "Our best minds," I say, "invent the hydrogen warhead." "And the tea cozy," he says. I love Betterwheatling. Intelligence turns me on.

Betterwheatling has gone to his study to write another page or two, and I am on the way to mine when Winterneet easily dissuades me with the offer of a nightcap.

"Just one," I say. On the stairs we meet Pavlovenka cheering up Meyers, who's feeling low on his last night, and they come too. We pile nightcap onto nightcap.

A knock at the door.

"Come in," calls Winterneet.

Watch out, Lucinella, I think. I'm ripe for what used to be the seduction scene on the next page but one, so whom shall I bring in the door? Not Bert—we don't really like each other that much—and not Zeus, who arrived late this afternoon. He sat beside me at dinner. He's very nice. And a poet on top of everything. It was simpleminded of me to assume he must be simple because of his size, oh, and his beauty! I kept looking into my plate—love's tough enough without that too. How about someone I haven't met yet? They're always the best kind. Already the latch clicks; the door opens.

Betterwheatling, of course! "Finished Chapter 5," he says. Sit beside me, Betterwheatling, I yearn. The light reflecting off my spectacles catches the light from his. Betterwheatling has come and sat beside me, on the floor, and his arm inside the pea-green sleeve of his woolen sweater raises his glass beside mine through the long, talkative night. I keep telling Betterwheatling what to include and what to leave out of this book he is doing. It's called *A Decade of Poetry*. He keeps asking me if I've read this, or this, and I don't care if I haven't. I keep gesticulating hilariously. Why does he keep bothering to argue me around his little finger? Zeus came in for a drink and left. Meyers has passed out on the chaise longue and Pavlovenka went to her room an hour ago. Now Winterneet offers us the continued freedom of his study and goes next door to bed.

Betterwheatling sees me downstairs to my door, but his legs walk away from under him, so I see him upstairs to his. We go in for a nightcap. I embrace his chest of drawers, on which he keeps his bottles. Betterwheatling's drunken, unspectacled moonface floats laughing before me. "You want to go to bed with me," he says. "Of course!" I say laughing. I see what he means. "But I like my wife," says Betterwheatling, looking apprehensively into my face. I laugh out at the unlikely passage between us of these truths. (I told you that's what turns me on.) We have sat down on chairs that precisely front each other at some distance and from here on in you are to imagine our faces naked to each other—eyes wide, our mouths open with this propensity to laughter. "It's not your problem," I say, and he understands that I mean my wanting. "You can have it for a present. I'm *drunk!*" I say. "What will I do with it?" says Betterwheatling, frowning at my ankles. He says, "I'm a sensual man, but so bloody moral!" The juxtaposition moves me: I could choose to assume Betterwheatling is the kind who keeps a wife wrapped for safety around his own fake loins, but he's more lovable if I believe him sexy *and* loyal, and isn't that my own last, best hope? Betterwheatling stands up and walks toward me with his hand out for my glass. Betterwheatling brings me my drink. He perches on the arm of my chair. "Don't worry, Betterwheatling," I say. "This conversation isn't about anything except our having this conversation, don't you know that?" "I don't know that," he says. Betterwheatling is sliding into the seat beside me. There's no room for both of us to sit. His wife writes him every day and I'm sure her letters are funny. And so I know Betterwheatling and I aren't going to make love. I have stood up. It's good, isn't it, to be good? Or am I the faker? I stand leaning over Betterwheatling, and I tell him everything, and the hound of heaven could not stopper up the words falling out of my open mouth.

Betterwheatling sees me downstairs to my door, and I know it's not my doing, only because it hadn't occurred to me to close upon each other with a violence that knocks a "good god" out of his throat, or it might be "good grief." His teeth are in my mouth, so I take my mouth and hide it on his chest, saying, "Jesus!" or is it "gee whiz"? I'm kissing the pea-green sweater and now it is a problem of disengagement. I'm laughing because I'm sure I've never said "god bless you" to anyone before. I duck out under his arms.

Alone in my room I compose a couplet to conclude my poem with an embrace like two severed human halves yearning to grow back together. Though I can't stop the metaphor dripping blood, I can imagine it down to a trickle. What I can *not*, is let it alone. It is my credo that what can be felt can be translated into words, even this vacancy with which, for an incalculable period, my mind has been gaping can be written. I'm trying to correct this extreme sideways inclination of my waist before I fall out of the chair. What I must do is lie down. I carry paper and a sharpened pencil to bed. The world folds into sleep.

Mornings at Yaddo I wake puzzled by the disembodied choir chanting a single sustained note of plainsong. I yearn for the resolution and open my eyes and understand that on the superhighway beyond the rose garden, past the greenhouses, on the far side of the lilac hedge thick as the walls of a medieval citadel, a diesel truck is passing Paradise. Shreds of mist cling to the lake surface; below, black shoals of fish stand in suspension. "Like the Japanese fleet after Leyte," says Winterneet.

Bert and I walk into breakfast at the same moment. "So," he says. "Am I going to make it into your bed?" The back of my head knows: Betterwheatling is walking into the room. "I shouldn't suppose so," I say. Bert says, "No, I suppose not." I say, "I haven't had a chance yet to look at your manuscript." Bert says, "You don't have to. I don't give a damn."

Betterwheatling comes and stands beside me at the sideboard, where I'm waiting for my toast to pop. He smiles with an odd black cast I have not seen in his eyes before. "You look terrible!" I say. Betterwheatling says, "The trouble with dissipation is it ruins the next morning's work." I say, "By the way, don't worry, you know." He says, "Worry about what?" And I understand that if we're not going to be playing together, neither are we going to talk it up.

"Betterwheatling, that's not fair," I say. "A man your size and sophistication, a New Yorker! If you're going to be honorable, that will really turn me on." From behind his glasses, Betterwheatling regards me with this new black smile.

This morning everybody lingers over breakfast. We keep pouring coffee into our cold cups: no one can bear to say goodbye. "We won't say goodbye, Meyers," we say. "We will see you before you leave." But when he comes down with his typewriter and bags, there's only Betterwheatling reading *The New York Times* and I, taking my lunch from the shelf. A car horn bleeps. The two men shake hands. I taste the male softness of Meyers's cheek. By the time we unembrace, he's already grown transparent. Betterwheatling is asking me for drinks in his study at 5:15, he'll leave a note for Winterneet and Zeus, he says, so we don't see Meyers walk out the door, climb into his taxi, and drive off between the giant pines and around the blue spruce, where he drops out of this world. By dinnertime, they'll have removed his chair. We won't mention his name. Tomorrow, when they put a new poet in his room, his memory will stir and we'll resent the new man for a night and a day—by then he will have grown into his place. In another week it will be me phoning for the cab to drive me around the giant pines, out onto the superhighway, through the village to my train. At the end of the rainbow is Grand Central Station, and by that time they will have removed my chair and be sitting down to dinner.

Betterwheatling and I saunter along the drive together. I look down at the quarter inch of chill white morning air which he deliberately keeps between his arm and mine and understand. *It is all a matter of the light.* By the thunder in my pulse I know: the Muse has struck, and in the blinding shock of the illumination I see how everything fits, the application of what I know, the relevance of anything that anybody says today, tomorrow, and for days to come. And so I do not see Betterwheatling turn down the path. I go into my study and write:

After dinner, in my poem, Pavlovenka stops the general movement into the drawing room by saying, "Aren't we going in the garden to see the surprise?" Betterwheatling and Winterneet, who are talking, change direction and follow her out of the door, drawing Bert behind them. He keeps saying, "What *is* this?" Lucinella is full of foreboding. The sun's gone in, and the mosquitoes have come out and make a straight line for the blood of the red-haired poet. Pavlovenka, distressed by the slowness of their progress through the wet evening grass, keeps saying, "Come on! We're not telling what! Lucinella and I cleared away the leaves," she says. "There! Put your head way in." Winterneet and Betterwheatling duck and look in briefly at the irregular mounds of dirt, some potting shards. Only Lucinella knows: *It's a matter of the light.* Bert bends, looks in, says, "Jesus H . . . ." and, beating at the retinue of insects that attends his head, turns after the others, who are already walking back in the direction of the house. Betterwheatling, let me catch your eye! A man who knows a tea cozy when he sees one will understand what's happened here. But Betterwheatling is asking Winterneet about his English publisher. Bert lifts his eyes first to the heavens, then to me, and says, "What the shit is this? I mean, what is this?"

The sparkling scene outside my window and all persons, affections, libido, arrogance and abjection, and every credo, even the passion to be read, have folded away. The staid, middle-aged housemaid in white linens leans her ear to my door, hears a pencil moving across paper, and steals away on plimsolled feet. She will return later to make my bed.

11

The bell rings. Outside my door stands the man I have never met before, in a jacket and tie, skinny, glasses, with a briefcase. He says he is William.

"Who?" I say.

"William," he says, "from Yaddo! I came the evening before you left, don't you remember, we sat on the pink couch and talked about Margery Kempe?"

"Margery *who?* Oh! Are you the one who got Meyers's old room?"

He doesn't remember.

"I'm sorry about all the mess and my clothes on the floor," I say. Maybe he won't notice my panties by his foot—and anyway, aren't we all siblings in our underwear?

He says he's come down from Yaddo to research the financing of a pilgrimage and his bus doesn't leave till midnight. He's taking his jacket off. The back of his neck is skinny.

"It's just the floor scrapers coming in the morning, early," I say. "I've got to clear everything away. What time is it?"

"I will help you," he says. He follows me into the kitchen.

"I'm sorry about all the dishes out, I'm reorganizing my shelves from scratch . . . where did I put the liquor?"

"Did you know you had to bring enough wine, cheese, and chickens to last you all the way to Jaffa, also your own frying pan?" he says, walking behind me round my narrow New York kitchen. We keep bumping and saying, "Sorry!"

"I'm sorry I keep wobbling," I say. "I've been up since seven, stopping the painter from putting burnt sienna in my white to give it body which *I* want pure, but he said it wouldn't cover and besides, nobody could tell the difference, which only makes it *worse!*" I say in the hope of an imminent grammatical solution. I tend to chatter with people I've just met. "One couldn't bear," I add, "to wake mornings knowing there was something in one's white!"

"Exactly!" he says. "After Margery's husband finally agreed to take the oath of chastity with her, God told her to wear white, quite against medieval custom for a married woman, and Margery'd had fourteen babies." His voice echoes in my living room, bare except for the inoffensive if undistinguished rectangle of my studio couch, which will do to sleep on, till I find my true bed. I eat and write on a drawing table whose unvarnished pine and honest cranking mechanism I can respect.

"I don't have a chair, I'm sorry. Sit on the couch. Dump the papers on the floor. I'll file them away."

"Sit here a moment," he says, patting the bedspread beside him, but I say I like sitting on the floor. "What time is it?"

Did I know pilgrims had to bring their own beds, he asks. "While they were laying in supplies in Venice, poor Margery got horribly on her fellowship's nerves, sitting there in her white clothes, abstaining from meat, while they were tucking in—any reference to Christ's passion made her roll around the floor 'crying and roaring boisterously.' What they wanted, in the worst way, was to *lose* her. Come embarkation day, they creep out of the inn, way before dawn, and bring their paraphernalia on board, and there, with her chickens and her mattress and her frying pan, on her knees, praying Jesus to forgive them, is Margery Kempe! She must be *the* pain in the ass in all of English literature. Mind if I get myself another drink?"

"Me too," I say. "One more and then I'll start clearing away."

"I wish," he says, coming back and sitting down beside me on the floor, "that I were a playwright, so I could have Margery's voice going as the curtain rises, never stopping throughout the first act, coming over the public-address system all during intermission, still yakking as she takes her final curtain call."

"Hey, that's funny, William! That's nice!" I really like that. I get up and pick my underpants, a shirt, a woolen cap, two pairs of socks off the floor. I perch on the edge of the couch. William is telling me about the time Arundel himself summoned Margery, accused of Lollardy, "for which, as you know," he says, "you could get your ass burned at the stake, and *she* scolds *him*, if you please, because his soldiers are using dirty language in the courtyard!"

I've learned how to keep my mouth shut in a curve of intelligent attention, though if I knew who Arundel was, my head, I think, would be slightly less cocked. I adjust the angle. I set my underpants, shirt, etc., back on the floor because there *is* no other place to put them. William has gone to get us another round of drinks. I curl on the couch, but now he sits down on the floor and tells me stories of medieval churchmen and politicos on the assumption they're acquaintances of mine as well, which is sweet of him.

"And Margery!" he says. "A middle-class mystic and

hysteric of mediocre mind and vulgar imagination with a genuine passion for a probably nonexistent God, making lifelong public relations out of the genuine persecution suffered for his sake. Don't you love paradox!"

"I do!" I say. "I love it!" I'm trying to control my eyes' tendency to pitch and roll in their sockets by focusing upon the yellow of the chevron on the ankle of William's navy-blue sock. I lean over the couch to bend closer and closer and I know: I am in the presence of Beauty.

William says, "My wife killed herself a year ago," and sobs briefly, not the way I do, *into* myself, but with his neck stretched like a dog's, so I slide down to the floor. My shoulder thrills at the touch of the shoulder of this man acquainted with grief, but he has pulled away and stands up. "Did I perform that little act," he says, "to make you come and sit beside me?"

I follow him out into the kitchen. He says, "I've missed my bus, you know that."

I know that.

"Can I sleep on your couch?" is what I think he said, but I was clanking the bottles I was putting up on the corner shelf, which isn't tall enough for the quarts, so I take them down again, listening intently for him to say it again.

He says, "I've got enough money for the bus back *or* a hotel."

Somewhere in all this mess there must be a towel.

William goes into the bathroom. I try the bottles on the shelf near the stove.

When I hear him moving in the living room, I go into the bathroom. I keep brushing and brushing my teeth because I don't know if I'm supposed to put my nightgown on. All he said was, can he *sleep* on my couch, if that *is* what he said, except what else does one put on, at night?

I go in. He's naked, I can tell, under my sheet. He says, "That's a pretty nightgown. Take it off."

"Then put out the light," I say.

"Why?"

"My nose is too long."

He's laughing. In the darkness, in my bed, I meet warm cool male skin, a bush of bristle here, and here.

"Don't you know I only came to see you?" he says.

I don't know that.

He laughs.

"What?"

"I was thinking," he says, and laughs again.

"*What*?" I say. I'm busy.

He says, "What if you're a bad poet . . . "

"Put on the light," I say, and leap out of bed. Somewhere in this pile is the last poem I've written, which might be the best thing I have ever done. William jumps out on his side. "Where's my briefcase? I hope I brought the one in which Margery and Jesus whisper in a corner, and she tells him how everybody is mean to her and Jesus says, never mind, he loves her better than all his other saints put together, and promises her everlasting life. Here."

We prop each other's manuscript before us, on the pillow. William wraps his foot around my ankle and we read.

I laugh.

"Where?" he says, looking over my shoulder.

I read him his witty line. (This is no moment to mention the weakness in his second stanza.)

He says, "You're *good!*"

"I *am?*" I touch my lips to his shoulder. He throws my poem in the air and turns out the light. I can tell he is enthusiastic. I wrap my hand around the back of William's neck to protect it from my memory of its meagerness.

The bell keeps ringing in this black velvet well in which I am luxuriously asleep.

The floor scrapers!

"Coming!" Blissfully the ringing stops and is replaced by the impatience outside my front door while I cannot and cannot find my housecoat in this mess.

"William? They will have to move the couch, *Will*iam."

"Right," William says, and opens his eyes, but I can see he's still asleep. Sleeping, he rises out of the sheets.

"Bathroom thataway, William, you're going to need clothes!"

"Right," he says.

"I'm sorry about all this mess," I say to the floor scraper—asthmatic, middle-age belly, tired hair into the forehead. "That's all right, miss, we'll do it in no time flat." Nice face! I tend to like people when they're walking in my doorway. And I like the young one too, big, round little head. He's hauling the machinery into my foyer. He upends my couch. The old man fills his arms with underwear. "Put it in the bathroom, miss?"

"Yes, please. No. Not the bathroom. Dump it on the kitchen floor. Just leave me room so I can make coffee. Would you like some?"

No, thank you. What they would like is to get on, and go home.

"Give you a nice gloss only needs buffing?" yells the old man over the whirring whine of the machine, so hugely out of proportion with the size of my room and the capacity my ears have to take it in, I cannot believe it. All day I will keep thinking they're about to turn the volume down.

"No gloss," I yell. "Leave the wood natural, please."

"You want a nice matte finish?" he shouts.

"No finish," I shout back.

"Just sealer, then, and wax it?"

"No wax, no sealer," I yell. I point where the revolving blades are milling dirt, varnish, and the top layers of wood into a fine-grade powder, exposing the beautiful raw grain. "Leave it like that," I yell.

"Dirt'll grind right in the open pores," shouts the floor scraper. "You got to put sealer."

"No sealer," I shout back.

William comes out of the bathroom, hair wet, shirt open at the throat, looking nice behind the cloud of powdered matter, which cannot be good for the poor floor scraper's lungs. He's wheezing. I try to imagine hungering for breath. A poem: "Death of a Floor Scraper." I look affectionately at him, but he turns his head away. I irritate him, I know. He looks toward William, who leans his back against the wall, slides into a squat, and goes back to sleep; the floor scraper turns toward his assistant, who keeps pushing the hellmachine, making a beautiful new furrow.

"It isn't that I don't think you're perfectly right!" I say, ashamed to be making such a fuss. I try to imagine world starvation, destruction, I visualize that final mushroom cloud, but at the still, hard center of my heart what I want, what I must have, is my wood left natural. I can't explain to the floor scraper, because I myself don't know that I believe that when I've got a chest of drawers for my clothes, found the right shelf for the bottles, and have filed each paper according to its kind, there will *be* no dirt, neither shall moth nor rust corrupt.

My ears shatter, my throat burns with dust and my eyes with the lack of sleep. Coffee! I climb over the upended couch in my kitchen door, where presently I see William standing with his tie on, mouthing a long sentence ending in O, I think. I put my hand behind my ear, meaning, "What?" He throws his right hand out, meaning, "Never mind." "Coffee?" I holler. "What?" He puts his hand behind his ear.

I wake from an indeterminate period in which I've stood staring into the black coffee in my cup, like a horse sleeping on its feet.

Where's William?

I climb over the couch into the foyer. Behind the noise and mist, over by the front door, in a jacket and tie, skinny, glasses, with a briefcase, a man beckons.

I draw back from his alien kiss. "Walk me to the elevator," he yells in my ear.

"Did you know," he asks me, "that it would take a month across Europe, on muleback, to visit Emperor Constantine's holy thumb, or one or another of the two heads of St. James the Less, or a piece of the true sponge that had touched the lips of Christ crucified?" The doors open, close. The elevator has carried him away.

I call my friend Ulla on the phone. Did she know, I ask her, that you had to bring your own frying pan, mattress, and chickens to last you all the way to Jaffa? "This guy I met at Yaddo came down to New York to research the financing of a pilgrimage. And he stayed over," I say. (How do the girls in commercials formulate their words while their mouths are smiling?)

"He stayed over?" says Ulla, her voice smiling too. Ulla is my best friend.

"A poet," I say, "called William. Ever heard of him?"

Ulla says, "No. Is he any good?"

"Oh *yes!*" I say, "except for a weakness in the second stanza. He says he only came to see me," I say, helplessly smiling.

The floor scrapers are gone. The new silence holds in suspension the stuff this world is made of ground back to its *ur*-particles.

Monday I sit cross-legged, at the heart of chaos, putting the canceled checks of years past in chronological order. I'm having a good time.

Tuesday I file Art. The soap operas I write evenings go in a pink folder. Mornings I write poetry, which I subdivide into the poem that won a prize, which goes into a blue folder tied with a ribbon; abandoned ideas I put in a black one, and those on which I am at work in green, isn't it, for hope?

Wednesday I call Ulla on the telephone. Aren't men who sleep over supposed to write or call?

Ulla, like the good friend she is, thinks up a score of reasons, all flattering to me, why William hasn't.

Thursday I file People. Letters of business go in a gray folder. I put Ulla and Winterneet and the note Betterwheatling tacked on the table at Yaddo asking me to drinks at 5:15 in a red folder labeled FRIENDS. I meant to weed out correspondence of no intrinsic interest from people I don't even like, but I can't put old Mrs. Winterneet into the wastebasket just because she fails to amuse me! (If I preserve you, will you, by sympathetic magic, hold on to me?) I put Mrs. Winterneet in a manila folder for ACQUAINTANCES.

Now, my correspondence with my editor requires some interesting discriminations. Does his first letter go into the purple folder labeled PEOPLE I HAVE NEVER MET, where I've put the fan letter from that man in Boston? And his second letter, after we had lunch, does that go into manila for ACQUAINTANCES? And after *that*, does he go into the gray folder for BUSINESS or the red one for FRIENDS? Into FRIENDS retroactive to the first letter? Then, after we quarreled, would he go back in the gray file? Retroactively? I don't think you can file ENEMIES (what color?) until you have a minimum of three or four. Now that we've made up, I'll put him in the red.

I'm sitting on the floor arranging each letter chronologically within its category when the bell rings. It's the mailman. A card, postmarked Yaddo. It says:

Oh Westron wind when wilt thou blow
the small rain down can rain
Christ that my love were in my arms
And I in my bed again.

I bring it to my lips, but I've run out of folders—what color is William when friendship is already red, and he's no friend—we never even got acquainted. I don't think one can have a folder for . . . No. That's not nice! I stand in the middle of the floor holding a lover's unfilable postcard between thumb and forefinger, and morning passes into evening, night into day, until the bell rings.

It's William, a man with a skinny neck and glasses, of no interest to me whatsoever, walking into my foyer. I say, "I'm sorry about the mess." He drops his briefcase. I'm kissing the edge of a lapel, blinded with emotion, I suck a button.

Morning. Where's William?

No one in the kitchen; the bathroom is empty, but as in the fairy tale, the dream has left a token: a damp towel is scrumpled on the towel rack.

The doorbell rings. It's William with his suitcases.

"Put your things on the floor, I guess, till I find us a chest of drawers, and you'll have to get colored folders and organize your papers," I say. So we are going to live together, are we, William and I! And sleep skin to skin, nights, Christ, yes—and all day we'll write poetry knee to knee. Walter Pidgeon and Marie Curie sitting across from each other, discovering uranium late into the night, leaning back, smiling wordlessly into each other's eyes.

"I don't even like him *that* much," I tell Ulla on the telephone. But Ulla says, "You like him." Her voice is smiling. Ulla is an expert on things like that. She's writing a novel called *Poets and Lovers*.

William is lying on the couch with his shoes on the white bedspread. There's nothing one can say, of course. Now he's taking them off. He says, "Come over here." He's taking his socks and his pants off, and his glasses. From here on in, this naked William, double-exposed upon the man in the jacket and tie framed in my doorway, like an old acquaintance in a fading snapshot, wakes mornings in my bed reaching for his glasses. I fill the air with the black smell of coffee, I'd coddle him an egg if I could find a pan. We have our breakfast out, then William goes back to write. I take the bus downtown. I can't work till I have everything in order.

"I'm looking for the perfect paper for my kitchen shelves," I say to the man behind the Contact paper counter.

"If you don't find it here, it probably doesn't exist," he says. Brown suit, face of a failed ambassador; from the islands of stubble in the creases of his cheek I deduce a wife in a nylon robe who packs him overripe bananas in his lunch bag every day. The Contact paper man despises bananas and never brings back the plastic Baggies, though she's asked and *asked* him. I rub the Contact paper salesman's back with glue and stick him in a poem called "The Contact Paper Salesman."

Is it okay to do this with a fellow human being?

He says, "We have stipples, speckles, spots, and circles, and our dots have Op effects. Here are the abstracts, conversationals, and florals, or if you like traditional, there's a fleur-de-lis, lotus, willow, and tartans, which we personalize in decorator colors, custom-keyed to your own home. Here's lace. Here's flocking you can't tell from cut velvet, and blue-jean regular or faded, with a real fabric feel. I can take a special order for your monogram, no extra cost, six weeks' delivery.

"We carry genuine marble reproductions and wood grain better than a tree, just sponge off with soap and water. I can show you our Famous Artists Series, actual brush strokes. Here's Van Gogh, here's the Lascaux Caves, or the Cimabue crucifix before the flood. Our man's in Chartres this moment, putting the stained glass on transparencies. In the eventuality of a nuclear disaster, you can glue your own rose window. We were first with environmentals, look at this seashore with a tie-in to our book department, 20 percent off an illustrated dictionary of crustaceans."

"I'll take plain white, please," I say.

"That'll run you twenty cents a square foot higher."

"Okay," I say.

"And we don't carry it," he says.

"I'll give you a special order," I say.

He says, "It's been discontinued. There's no demand. If I had it here, in my hand, I wouldn't sell it to you, you'd be back next week complaining it showed every speck of dirt."

I say I'll think about it and I'll be back. The Contact paper salesman's eyelids click shut and register "No Sale." His flat cheek infinitesimally sags: the Contact paper salesman has grown five minutes older. Already he has forgotten me.

I take the elevator to the furniture department and visit the chair I cannot afford. I touch the wood. Its temperature adjusts to my blood. My finger follows the slightest shift in the direction of the carver's tool. The carver sits in my soul with his back to me (centuries divide us; and he's never Jewish). He carved these armrests like two halves of an embrace that opens courteously outward, before terminating into formal scrolls.

I take the elevator down to stationery and buy a dozen pencils.

Is that stout odd body in the striped stockings waving at *me*? "Pavlovenka! I didn't recognize you! What are *you* doing out of Yaddo?"

Pavlovenka says she saw me upstairs, in the furniture department, and called me by name, but I was stroking a chair and she tiptoed away. And what am I working on, she asks.

I tell Pavlovenka about my poem called "Euphoria in

the Root Cellar," which I've just finished. She shrieks with the deliciousness of the coincidence: a student in her freshman class is writing just such a poem, about a poet writing a poem in his poem!

"Mine's different!" I cry. What I need is a brand-new notebook for a poem I am going to be doing that will be so different, literature will never be the same again.

William is glad to see me. "Lucinella, where's the bourbon?"

"Oh!" I say. "I moved the bottles to the shelf near the refrigerator."

"I'm hungry," says William. "Let's go out and eat."

"How can I eat!" I cry. "I bought a notebook and twelve new pencils."

"So, let's sit down and write."

But how can I write with chaos breathing in my ear, yearning for just such a crack, such a fault in the system, to come creeping back among my papers? I must find the place, quickly, to put my new notebook, and here is exactly the right white folder. I'm surprised! There are two notebooks, both blank, already in it, and now I remember the time I was going to write this new and completely different poem which needed a brand-new notebook, and buying one and bringing it home and putting it into this white folder. I remember my surprise at finding a new notebook already in it and remember remembering needing, buying, bringing, and putting it in a white folder.

"William, when are *you* going to organize *your* papers?"

"My papers," William says, "are in an ascending and descending order of non sequitur."

"That's funny, William." I like that. I kiss him. He says, "Come and lie here," but how can I make love so long as there's disorder among my pencils.

I sit in the middle of the floor sharpening the twelve

new pencils to precision points, each one exactly equal in length to each of the eleven others.

What is this straining, almost a rasping, in my chest? It's the pain of the discrepancy between Walter Pidgeon sitting upright and William lying down on the couch again.

I go and kneel by William. I untie his shoes and rub his feet for him and say, "William, be a love, don't put your shoes on the white bedspread, the damn thing costs four bucks to dry-clean."

"More feet rubbing," William says. (Mark down the day, a Thursday, on which it is established I can tell William what to not do: the future is all before us.)

"And straighten out your towel on the towel rack," I say.

"If I remember," says William, "I will."

"Try to remember, William," I say, "that a scrumpled towel cannot dry, and William, why do you lie down instead of sitting up when you're writing?"

"Because, Lucinella, we don't have a chair," William says.

"That's true," I say.

Next day the bell rings.

Outside my door is a man with a chair upholstered in turquoise crap with tulips, quilted in gilt thread.

"You have the wrong address!" I scream, but he shows me the label:

To:
Lucinella,
New York.
I love you,
William

"William, could you imagine that for some people an ugly object can cause physical distress, like a bad smell?"

"Yes," says William. William has a good imagination. We lie on the couch together and I tell him my theory that kitsch is visited upon our generation because of Adam's second disobedience in swallowing the core of that apple, though god knows god did his damndest to keep us from the knowledge that his secret name is I AM NOT and the corollary nonexistence of our souls exemplified in the stupidity of the proportions, the dishonesty of shape, the venal color and fabric of this kind of furniture, so would William please always put the chair in that corner when it's not in use?

"Okay," says William.

Why doesn't he mind? Next day I take the bus downtown to buy myself a leather belt, and put it on under my blouse. I take the elevator to the furniture department—my chair's still here. I ride down to stationery. There's this poem I am going to write, for which I need a brand-new notebook. At home I find the right white folder to put it in. Surprise!

I go into the bathroom and find William's towel scrumpled on the towel rack. I make my first notch in my belt for straightening it out without a word, and a second one, next day, because I keep my mouth shut about the chaos in his papers. I'm surprised when my mouth opens and hollers, "Why is that chair not put back in the corner?"

"Because I'm sitting in it!" William shouts.

When our eyes retract into their sockets and the floor stops heaving, it has been established: William and I can yell at one another. (This is Saturday).

"Where, Lucinella, is the bourbon? Why is it never where it was?"

"Because, oh William, don't you understand that it is searching for its Platonic shelf?"

Sunday.

"Lucinella, where's the chair?"

"I put it in the closet. William, can you imagine walking around all day with an ugly object continually in your peripheral vision? Will?"

"What?"

"How come you don't mind my nagging you?"

"Mind!" says William. "I hate it!" He unbuttons his shirt and shows me his leather belt. Two notches Thursday. One, when I nagged him to straighten out his towel in the bathroom, and one to please put the chair back in the corner. Four Friday: one chair in the corner, one shoes on the bedspread, and two scrumpled towels. Saturday—

"Hold everything!" I cry, and show him my notches for all the times I kept quiet. "William? I've often wondered, why *don't* you straighten out your towel on the towel rack?"

"Never occurs to me," he says.

"You think you ever will straighten it?"

"Probably not," William says. "Lucinella," he says, "will you marry me?"

Ulla calls me on the telephone. "And *when*," she asks, "am I going to meet your William?'

"As soon as I get everything in order, we'll have a party," I promise.

"How will I ever get everything in order!" I ask William. "As soon as I get one thing straightened out, *you* come and mess it up again, you scrumple up your towel, your papers are in chaos, and you lie with your shoes on the white bedspread instead of sitting up when you write, William, how come *you do everything wrong all the time?*"

"Which reminds me, Lucinella, what's happened to the chair?'

"I put it in the basement."

"First you made it stand in a corner, now you've nagged it clear out of the house!"

"William? How come you never nag me?'

"What about?" asks William.

"Whatever you can't stand about me."

William is thinking. "When you keep nagging I sometimes want to murder you, but I can *stand* it."

"Why don't you tell me to straighten out *my* towel on the rack?'

"Because I don't care if it's scrumpled."

"But, William, a scrumpled towel cannot dry!"

"Lucinella, sweetheart, love! A dry towel does not move my imagination!"

"Nag me. Go on," I say.

William looks harried. "You're a slob," he says.

"No, I mean something true about me. Go on."

"You are a true slob," William says.

"A slob, William! I! Who can neither eat nor write nor love so long as my house is not in perfect order, how am I a slob?'

"Your towel is scrumpled in the bathroom. Lucinella, I don't care—"

"Ah, but," I say, "that's different, don't you see, that's only because I haven't got around yet to straightening it out. Nag me some more."

"The kitchen," says William, "is in such a shambles we have to eat out."

"Only till I find the right Contact paper," I explain, "which they no longer manufacture. Go on."

"Lucinella, I don't give a good goddamn, but, sweetheart, *why* is your underwear all over the floor?"

"Tomorrow I will go downtown and find us a beautiful old chest with the right drawer for each category of clothing."

"Meanwhile," says William, "may I just wipe the black smudge off your nose?"

"Leave it!" I say. "I'm saving it. First, I have to get

things on their proper shelves in the kitchen and you have to file your papers, and when the house is in order there will be a Great Washing. Oh, William, my face and hands will be as pink as new soap, I'll brush my hair, exercise, eat the right foods, learn French. William, you won't recognize it's me!"

I call Ulla on the telephone. "I'll probably marry William. Ulla?" I say because I can't hear her smiling.

Ulla says, "Great!" She asks me if I've heard about this new and completely different magazine published by this guy Maurie. "I want you to meet him," she says.

"I want you to meet William!" I say. "We'll have a party."

"Maurie," Ulla says, "has fantastic taste. He can smell a good poem."

"So can William. William can—"

"Winterneet says Maurie is the best editor in town. You should see the list of his contributors," and Ulla keeps on keeping on about this Maurie. I feel the bitterness of deprivation.

That is the moment, while I'm talking to Ulla and my back is turned, that chaos gets his foot in the door. William is lying on the couch with his shoes on the white bedspread, very excited. He says he's writing a poem called "The True Slob," about a perfectionist in a chronic state of desperation, and he's using *one of my pencils!*

He's shocked at the way I howl. "You don't understand anything," I mumble, sitting on the floor and feverishly sharpening the eleven other pencils to precisely equal the diminished length. One breaks. Rapidly, so my left hand won't know it, my right drops it in the garbage, where William finds it the next day and says, "Look, Lucinella, a perfectly good pencil in the garbage."

I put my head down, crying in despair. William takes me in his arms. "Lucinella! Sweetheart! What's the matter?"

"You!" I say. William strokes my hair. "Me. Everything!" He kisses my forehead. I am weeping disconsolately. "Both our towels are scrumpled in the bathroom, one pencil is shorter than the eleven others, and the black lead from the shavings is all over the floor, and my new filing system doesn't work! I've lost my editor. I can't figure out what color he is in."

"Why don't you file him alphabetically?" William suggests. "Lucinella, don't. Why are you tearing up your colored folders? Don't throw them in the garbage! Lucinella, where are you going?"

"Downtown, to get myself a brand-new set from A to Z. I'm starting from scratch," I say.

The doorbell rings.

It's the Fuller brush man, coat flapping. He looks exhausted. His tie is knotted like a rope around his neck; his eyes pop.

"I'm sorry," I say, "but I was on my way downtown."

The Fuller brush man says he has a present for me. "Free sample of Paradise Cleaner. Spray, wipe, and it stays wiped once and for all."

"Which," and I smile into the Fuller brush man's beautiful protruding eyes, "you and I know to be morally impossible."

"Millions in research have been sunk into perfecting this scientific miracle. Let me demonstrate." He's walking into my foyer.

"I'm sorry about the mess . . . "

The Fuller brush man addressees an area of floor the size of a man's fist. "Spray and watch."

William comes and squats beside me. We watch the

wetness glisten before seeping down into the layers of dust, street dirt, household droppings, and pencil shavings which I've been ripening on my floor against the day of the Great Cleaning.

"Wait," he says, "and wipe."

I wipe, I rub, scrub, scrape. "We didn't wait long enough," I say to console the Fuller brush man. "Maybe it's because I didn't let the floor scraper put on sealer, the dirt's ground right into the open pores."

The Fuller brush man takes a plastic bag out of his sample case and says, "This is dirt. Throw some on the place we sprayed. Go on," he says. "More, don't be shy. The molecular structure of Paradise has been altered so it will repel the neutrons of dirt into eternity. It is a scientific impossibility for dirt ever to settle here again."

"Capillary action," says William, as we watch the wetness seep upward. It has fused my and the Fuller brush man's dirt to the consistency and color of mud.

"How much," I ask, "would it take to do this floor?"

"Including the foyer?" The Fuller brush man squints his eyes to make an educated estimate. "Gallon would do it at a pinch, gallon and a half is ample!" He takes out his order book, and lends me his ball-point pen. I sign over to him my common sense in return for which he guarantees me the millennium.

Thursday we visit Ulla. She's moved in with Maurie. "Lucinella!" she cries. "You're looking fabulous!" (I am? I'm trying for a glimpse of myself looking fabulous in the hall mirror behind Ulla, who is beautiful in shirt and jeans.) Now Ulla is shaking hands with William, now he turns to hang up his coat, now she must see the meagerness of the back of his neck.

"They're here! Maurie!" cries Ulla. Through a half-open door we can see a bed, the soles of a pair of shoes, a stomach on which stands a fat manuscript.

"He'll be out in a minute," Ulla says. "Come in. Sit. So! How *is* everything! Maurie?"

"Nice place," I say. "And so near the park!"

"Very," says Ulla. "So, how's everything! You're looking fabulous! Maurie! It's just this writer keeps bugging and bugging him about his manuscript."

"We know about writers! Ulla, let the poor man alone. Must be one hell of an undertaking to get out a magazine," I say, to cover for Maurie, for Ulla's sake, and for my sake too. If it is not his overwhelming duties that keep Maurie from leaping up to meet me, it would prove that I am not the kind of woman who compels mankind to its feet. Generations of men now alive will fail to come leaping when I've left William, and my old age will die of loneliness.

No, it won't! Here he comes, a snub-nosed, fat young man; his polished round face reflects light. His pale eyes, naked without brows or lashes, regard me through the two thick circles of his rimless lenses with a look of unusual intelligence. Trust Ulla to sleep only with what's best in the arts. Maurie says he wants to see some of my poems for his magazine. In the pause which follows, Maurie does not say he wants to see some of William's poems, seems not to see William, and William says, "When is your first issue coming out?"

"We've brought out two already," says Maurie.

"Must be one hell of an undertaking," I say.

"It's called *The Magazine*," says Ulla, "a perfectly new concept in publishing. It prints only what is genuinely new and excellent in contemporary writing."

"In contradistinction," says William, "to the kind of magazine which specializes in publishing what's phony, old hat, and second-rate?"

"In contradistinction," says Maurie, "to *all* others, whose editors have neither guts nor taste."

"Whereas *you* recognize the excellence that everybody else has missed?"

"That's right," says Maurie, with an extraordinary smile, showing the charming small gap between his two front teeth.

"However original the text," says William, "which, by definition, means without anything to which it can be compared, *you* always understand right away what it means, and how it works."

"Not always right away," says Maurie.

"In fact," William says, "confess. The less you understand, the more it turns you on. If it looks funny on the page, you run and publish it."

"I never run," says Maurie. "I'm fat, as you see. I have a slow metabolism, I like lying down. Reading gives me pins and needles and makes my scalp crawl, so when a manuscript looks like it might be good, I frown, I pretend I've fallen asleep. If I still feel myself airborne, I publish."

"And you are never wrong," says William, "never mistake a fad for a movement, hysteria for passion?"

"Every morning at 3 a.m. I wake and wonder what the hell I'm doing," says Maurie, smiling at me.

Ulla catches my eye, meaning: "Can you help liking him?" I'm trying to catch William's, meaning: "Cool it."

"And the world," William says, "will be so good as to suddenly produce this reservoir of genius for you to edit?"

"Oh, genius, my goodness!" Maurie says. He doesn't blink exactly. How would I put it into words, this passing shadow that has altered the light of Maurie's stare, meaning he has heard all this so many times before and always in a voice congratulating itself on its remarkable astuteness?

"Ulla, why don't you show us the apartment? Coming, William?"

"You go," he says. For William to get out of his chair presupposes he is sitting in it, which presupposes that he exists, and Maurie's failure to fully perceive him has called this into question. William must force his image to register on Maurie's vision and his words to take on substance in Maurie's imagination. William says, "So what's to be with poor old Meyers? His Pulitzer has done him in. He tells me he feels the world watching over his shoulder and can't write."

"I'm publishing a poem he's just finished in the next issue," says Maurie.

When Ulla and I return, William is sitting in his chair reading an advance copy of *The Magazine*. Maurie is lying on the sofa picking his nose behind a fat manuscript.

"Lunchtime! William! Maurie?"

Maurie is asleep.

"MauRIEEEEEE!"

Now Maurie remembers the call he's got to put through to the printer and carries his plate to the phone table in the hall.

Has it occurred to William that we *could* put our coats on and go home? And leave Ulla with the salad and quiche she's made specially for us, and the color rising into her head, and the increasing pitch of her conversation, in which I join her. We talk about lettuce and patty shells and the narrowness of New York kitchens, to cover Maurie's continued absence and the deepening dullness of William's silence, and after lunch maybe the two of them will sit and talk.

After lunch Ulla impales Maurie with a look. "The weather is fabulous, Maurie, let's go for a walk in the park!"

Maurie says, "Great, you do that, which will give me a chance to look over Winterneet's new poem before he arrives."

Now are we going to say, "Maurie, go to hell," and put on our coats and go home?

We put on our coats and follow Ulla into the park, and maybe when we get back, over coffee, Maurie will see how interesting William and I really are.

Ulla is pointing out the prospects. I say, "Fabulous! Great!" and "Oh wow!" but really I am staring down into my Underground, where I collect the men since Adam who have ignored me. The trouble is my face. It's not the kind that topples towers, Paris was quite right. And Lancelot wore Guinevere's favor on his sleeve instead of mine. It was Héloïse got Abélard! (I would have liked him.) It was for

Mrs. Simpson that a man gave up the British Empire. Even this grocery boy hiking his package up under his arm, as he waits for the light to change, does not bother to look and see me. I feel the draft from William's Underground and take his hand. He squeezes mine. Why can't one make that do?

When we get back, there's J. D. Winterneet, sitting with Maurie. He's pleased to see me. I can always tell. I introduce William. "I'm so pleased, sir, to meet you!" William says. Winterneet gives him his hand. "I'm sorry," he says, "I didn't catch the name."

Ulla brings coffee, which Maurie and Winterneet carry into the other room so they can work.

Maurie! Come back! One moment of your full attention would lift this curse and we could go home.

"Maurie! They're leaving!"

Maurie comes to the door promptly, takes my hand. "Remember, a couple to half a dozen of your poems, depending on the length. William, goodbye. We'll see you."

"See my ass," William says.

We walk holding hands. "Maybe I could send him the one where Margery has got to marry God the Father, though Jesus is the one she likes," says William. "Lucinella, do you love me?"

What, William, now? When you are yellowish, pinch-nosed, and chicken-necked? Snubbing does not become a man.

I kiss the sleeve of his jacket.

"Will you marry me?"

"Probably," I say.

The next day Ulla calls to say she thinks William is terrific.

"He *is?*" I say.

Is he, I wonder.

The poet goes to heaven. For three
weeks the choir of angels sings
his praises, then they take a
coffee break. The poet cries,
"Nobody loves me!"
Robert Pack

The bell rings. It's the mailman, for William. A note from *The Magazine*. William unfolds it and reads:

Margery and God terrifically funny.
If you can fix weakness in second
stanza let me see it again.
Maurie.

"William? What's the matter?" William is frowning. He says, "It's not his not accepting it. I couldn't care less. It *is* his magazine to publish in, or not, what he sees fit. It's the arrogance of 'Fix weakness'! I don't rate a definite article?"

"What he doesn't understand is my poetry depends on a certain looseness in some stanzas," William says. "And I'm *not*, Lucinella, going to his goddamn party!"

The bell rings. It's for William from *The Magazine*.

Terrific. Fall issue.
OK? M.

William is waiting for happiness, which does not occur.

"Bastard!" he says. "Two triple-spaced lines! I don't rate a letter of acceptance? Okay, okay. I guess we *have* to show up at the party."

IV

"Lucinella! Come in!" cries Ulla. "You're looking fabulous!" (So William said, but then he even wants to marry me.)

Ulla is wearing her harem pants and looks beautiful. She says William looks terrific, but there I *know* she's fibbing. "Dump your coats on the bed inside. Cilena! Come in! You're looking fabulous!"

Here comes Maurie, his fat face gleams. He puts an arm around my shoulder. I really like Maurie, but don't, Maurie, *please* don't ignore William, now look what you've done!

Maurie's snub has uncovered William's Underground and let out his company of little black familiars with their barbed and poisonous tails. One crawls out the bottom of his trouser leg and says, "You've got a weak second stanza and at Maurie's, Thursday, Winterneet didn't know who you were." Another falls out of his sleeve. It says, "Your poetry is worthless!" There's one clinging to his lapel, like a boutonniere, which says, "Remember Lila, who put out for the whole tenth grade except you and that kid with the adenoids? And your wife killed herself, no wonder Lucinella doesn't want to marry you!" And one, a meany, sits astride William's nose and regards him with the precise slant of eye Miss Colman, in kindergarten, wore seeing the pee puddling at his feet and William groans out loud.

"The trouble with Maurie," he says, "is he doesn't have the first idea what publishing is all about."

This is not true. I clasp my hands around William's arm and keep silent. And I add, "Also, he picks his nose." (So does William in private. So do I.)

William undoes my hands from around his arm and stalks after Maurie.

What I cannot forgive is the meagerness of the back of William's neck; tomorrow I'll tell him I want out. Tonight, while I'm looking fabulous, I'll practice operating solo again, and there's Meyers in the doorway.

Fondly we embrace. Ridiculous, we say, how we never get together! New York is impossible. We figure the year and month to the day we did the crossword at Yaddo, walked to the village, saw the Chinese lady's impossibly tiny shoe in the museum, drank beer all afternoon, and talked. "You watched the ball game," I say. "We ate peanuts." He says, "Next day was Monday and I went home."

We get drinks and sit down on the sofa, and that is our undoing.

"We saw Winterneet at Maurie's, Thursday," I say.

"The Betterwheatlings are here," Meyers says.

"Have you seen Bert?" I say.

"Pavlovenka," he says.

"Zeus," I mention. "So. What are you writing?"

"I'm not," says Meyers. His fingers tremble. His mustache droops. "You?" he asks me.

"A poem called 'The Bucket,'" I say, but the prospect of explaining brings on an extreme lassitude. I close my mouth.

Meyers's mouth is closed. I *like* Meyers. I want to frame a question to which his answer will be something true, preferably intimate, but a glutinous film is growing between my lips and I know if I don't part them my mouth will be sealed up forever.

(Over by the bar, at a tremendous distance, I see William talking to Maurie. From the way Maurie leans backward I know William is telling him what publishing is all about.)

Meyers's lips part. "Have you seen Winterneet?"

"At Maurie's, Thursday," I say.

(Maurie turns his back on William and walks away.)

"There's Winterneet!" says Meyers. And here's Maurie coming to greet his famous guest and I know what Meyers wants is to go talk to Winterneet, but he cannot get up from the sofa because he doesn't want to hurt my feelings. I want to go to William, who stands alone, holding his glass, but I cannot. I don't want to hurt Meyers's feelings, and now it is too late. Our rumps have put roots down into the sofa. Here Meyers and I will sit in mutual silence through eternity.

A hundred years pass. Benjamin, that princely man, climbs through the thickly growing crowd toward me. His eyes are friendly. He bends his beautiful and clever head, and kisses me on the cheek. I wake. I rise. My unsealed lips say, "Hi, Benjamin! I thought you were at Berkeley! You know Meyers, of course," I say, but Meyers is gone. A girl with glasses whose face needs a good wash points her eager nose into the space between Benjamin and me.

He says, "I couldn't leave New York. So? What are you writing?"

"A poem called 'The Bucket,'" I tell Benjamin and the bespectacled girl. "It asks the question, 'Why does one go to parties?'"

"I never go to them," a man says in passing.

"Who's that?" asks the bespectacled girl.

"Max Peters, the nasty critic," we tell her.

"I always throw up at parties" is what I think the girl says. "I come to have conversation and meet people, but I never talk to people I don't know and I don't know anybody so I never have any conversation or meet anybody."

"You will, at the *next* party," I say, meaning to include the elderly woman standing on my left.

"That's why I couldn't go to Berkeley," says Benjamin. "I might have missed the next party."

The girl looks at Benjamin and smiles and turns expectantly to me. She's lighted upon a conversation.

"We cannot leave New York," I say, "although the Bomb will get us if we stay." I don't want to keep turning my shoulder against the elderly woman, but Ben is saying, "By the way, what *is* it that's going to be happening at the next party?"

"*It!* The Great Orgasm," I say, but a swell in the nice noise of the growing party carries the sound away. Benjamin leans down his ear toward me. "Which?"

I raise my chin. "The Great Orgasm!" I shout with a false sense of déjà vu: we really *have* been here before, at the Betterwheatlings' party, Sunday. Benjamin's eyes quicken. He recognizes himself saying, "What's the use of that the morning after?"

"But, Ben, there *is* no morning after, not after the Great One," I return familiarly.

"Damn!" Benjamin says, "I've been to all the wrong parties."

"Of *course* you have! The right one is the one you're not at," I familiarly, comfortably say, and notice the guilty chill on my left side where the old woman's bulk no longer displaces air.

Behind me stands William, and says, "He runs that magazine like a shoe business."

I turn back to Benjamin. He's gone.

The bespectacled girl has disappeared.

"Lucinella!" says Winterneet, and takes my hand.

"J. D. Winterneet!" I say, pleased.

"How do you do, sir," says William.

Winterneet puts out his hand and says, "Winterneet. I'm sorry, I didn't catch your name. I'm too old for parties, Lucinella. Come and sit down on the sofa."

"Better not," I say, "because when we run out of things to say we will be stuck with each other for eternity."

I've made Winterneet smile. On my right, William's Underground gapes.

"We can go and freshen up our drinks," says Winterneet.

"That's what I mean! And there's always the john, but that means going clear out of the room and staying out and god knows what one may miss."

I've made J. D. Winterneet laugh.

"I'm writing a poem all about parties," I say, "which explains why we can't simply say, 'Thank you, now I've had enough of you and want to go and talk to someone else.' It's Courtesy which wisely constrains us, and by tacit contract you will treat me as if I mattered in return for vice versa, so that we keep the rug in place to cover the abyss under one another's feet." I tell Winterneet about my Underground, where I preserve the company of persons who have thought me less than perfectly interesting and charming, reinforcing my suspicion that they're right. I'm talking too much, I know, but Winterneet looks at me so kindly that from where I haven't figured floats up the highly unstable, rainbow-hued, transparent company of persons who like me, confirming my suspicion that I'm charming and interesting. I feel myself delicately taken under the armpits and borne upward: three quarters of an inch above the rug, I float.

"Now you've closed every avenue of our escape," says Winterneet smiling, "we're stuck with each other for eternity."

"Not if we keep standing up," I explain. "If we can

keep talking ten minutes longer, the room will have filled to capacity and we'll maneuver the quarter turn: you will accidentally turn an angle of ninety degrees and find yourself in the middle of the adjacent conversation."

I demonstrate and find myself looking into the clever eyes of the girl with the unwashed face.

"I've read everything you've written," she says. "It's exactly my cup of tea."

My eyes cross and focus on the bridge of her nose. I put on a falsely sweet, discouraging face and say, "*Thank* you! How nice."

She says, "I don't suppose praise gives you any fun any more." She has a small, sharp face, like a chicken with owl glasses, through which she looks out with a hungry hopelessness that makes me mean.

I say, "Hemingway says you can tell outsiders because they praise you to your face. There's no way to handle it."

She blushes. "I can't see you being at a loss," she says.

"Are you kidding!" I say.

"You know everybody," she says.

"So will you," I say, "after ten years of parties."

She shakes her head. "I never get invited. I don't know anybody."

"What brought you tonight?"

"Ten wild horses," I think she says.

"What?"

She says, "I fixated on this party: the Start of the New Life. But tonight I kept not getting dressed." Inside her brown, beautifully tailored woolen dress, she stands with rounded back and belly. She says, "I figured if I came late and left early I could survive an hour and a half." This girl, who says what she actually means, tends to mumble her words inside her mouth, so as to keep the option of eating them.

“What is your name?” I ask her.

“Lucinella,” she says.

“How old are you?”

“Twenty.”

“Hang in there, Lucinella. It gets better from here on in,” I say. “You’ll publish a poem” (young Lucinella shakes her head), “you will love a man” (she grimaces; she looks as if she’s going to cry). “When you make a faux pas, you won’t toss all night trying to unsay it.” (She laughs out.) “You’ll fatten up to accommodate your nose, you’ll wash your face, you’ll learn how to wear your hair—give it ten years.”

“Ten years!” howls young Lucinella. The decade to which I cling by a fingernail, with my legs streaming horizontally behind me, feels to her like a drafty waiting room without a clock, when you’re not sure the trains are running. “For god’s sake, go and get yourself a drink,” I tell her.

“Liquor makes me throw up,” she says.

“Well,” I say, “I guess I’ll go and freshen mine.”

I pass William telling Maurie J. D. Winterneet’s poems are old-hat and Maurie says, “Don’t be a ninny, William,” and walks off.

There’s that old woman standing in a small clearing in the crowd, holding her glass. I will go talk to her, and by sympathetic magic next time I’m in a hole at a party someone will rescue me. But Betterwheatling is walking toward me and I remember I am in love with him. It’s just I never think of him from one party to the next.

“How’s *A Decade of Poetry* coming?” I ask him. The last time we talked about it, at Yaddo, we ended kissing on the stair.

Betterwheatling tells me the fuck-up with his publisher, in detail. It is not interesting.

“By the way,” I say, “who’s the old woman in the frizzy hair putting on her coat?”

"That's old Lucinella, the poet," says Betterwheatling. "She hasn't written much in these last years. Used to be good in a minor way."

"How can she bear it!" I say. "To be old, and minor!"

Betterwheatling and I watch Maurie and Ulla coming to make a small fuss at her leaving.

Still, Betterwheatling stands beside me. His proximity moves me.

"You have an English publisher?" I ask him.

Betterwheatling tells me in detail about the fuck-up with his English publisher.

Maurie joins us. I say, "Doesn't Ulla look terrific?"

"Terrific," says Maurie, in the voice detective-fiction writers used to describe as "dry."

Ulla sits on the sofa, her back straight, feet neatly side by side, her lips parted to receive what William, who squats before her, is telling her. (I'm surprised anyone would flirt with William, till I remember I'm probably going to marry him.) He's telling her the history of his publications, from the first acceptance of his poems by the college paper, of which he was the editor, to the latest contretemps with Maurie at *The Magazine*. He has a childlike trust in Ulla's full participation.

Ulla sees Maurie and me watching, and smiles demurely.

Maurie performs a quarter turn, sees young Lucinella, and says, "I'm publishing your poems."

"You are!" she says. The world has stopped spinning. Only her head continues to revolve. She suspects a hoax: Maurie is trying to cheer her up!

Maurie says, "I do have some quibbles—"

"Don't think I don't know," she says quickly, "that metapoetry's been done and been done. It's coy to be writing one's poems in one's poems."

"Yes," says Maurie, "but what I want to say is—"

"My metaphors don't dovetail," says young Lucinella.

"Please to shut up a moment," Maurie says, "so I can think. What I mean is, it's okay for the narrator to mock her heroine if that's her nature, but is it okay for the writer to be so unkind? To out-truth truth is one way of lying."

"That's true!" cries young Lucinella, intensely elated. "You're right! It's like trying to seduce the reader by saying, 'Look at mine, which is the same as yours,' which isn't even true. And no one loves you the better!"

Maurie says, "There you go again. Why 'seduce'? *Is* that what you're doing?"

"No," she says, "but I thought I'd say it first so you won't."

Betterwheatling's disappeared. In his place stands his wife, Cilena, who says, "I'm no good at parties."

I tell her about my poem about a party where people carry buckets to collect the odds and ends of love—attention, flattery, a proposition or two, a little rape. "The object is to keep your bucket brimful at all times."

"I know," says Cilena, and holds up hers.

I show her mine. "It's got no bottom. Say someone wants to marry you. In the act of putting him into the bucket, he's already fallen out the other end."

"So that you have to collect in perpetuity," says Cilena. "So *tire*some."

"*Why* do we?" I ask her.

"Ah," says Cilena, "I'm reading Erich Fromm, and he says we experience separateness as anxiety."

"Wow!" I say.

"I know," she says. "Not only anxiety, but as shame and guilt."

"The guilt of not being loved! Jesus . . . "

I tell her about the Great Orgasm. "You get fucked and stay fucked once and for all."

"The millennium!" says Cilena.

I tell an elegant black man who stands near us about the bottomless bucket. He thinks I'm flirting with him. He's right.

He says that this is precisely what he's working on. "I'm doing a piece for *The Magazine* on the parallel uses of attractiveness and power."

"*Are* you!" I say excitedly. "Power I never understand. Or is it another sort of bucket?" I turn to ask Cilena, but she's gone.

"Power is the *point*," he says, very excited too. "In the social animal, the powerful male has the selective advantage of the attractive female at the peak of her oestrus."

"Erich Fromm says we experience separateness as anxiety, and guilt, and shame," I tell him.

"It's a matter of genetic survival," he says, "because the weak am ale ad oes an otap ass aona his age nes."

I say, "I at hink awe a ar eal la loo kin ga fo rat hea mill en nium."

He says his name is Newman. He'll send me the article. We must have lunch and continue our discussion. He draws his head back, startled by the enthusiasm of my acceptance. He's gone.

Why is Betterwheatling wearing an overcoat?

"What's the matter, Betterwheatling?"

"I don't know," Betterwheatling says. "*Is* something the matter?"

"You look as if . . . " But I can't tell as if what Betterwheatling looks. I tell him my theory that being snubbed brings every abject memory crawling out of its Underground, but feeling liked makes the good ones float out of . . . goddamn, I've dovetailed my two metaphors! Now I can finish my poem! Out of the goddamn brimful bucket. Of course!

When I say damn a lot, I know I'm high, though not so

high I can't climb down if I want, only I can't seem able to want to. I tell Betterwheatling about the bottomless bucket. True, he says, lovers fall out the bottom, but friends tend to stay in. "Oh, Betterwheatling, that's true, but it ruins my theory." I tell him about Erich Fromm. He says if only Fromm would not write such awful English.

I tell Betterwheatling about the Great Orgasm, and how we come to parties to hunt the millennium.

"Nonsense," Betterwheatling says.

"Then, Betterwheatling, why *do* we go to parties? Why not the library? Why aren't we home cooking or out horseback riding?"

Betterwheatling says he was at the library all afternoon and is not a good cook. Horses, he doesn't like. He says he likes parties.

"Betterwheatling, if you're going to be commonsensical you're no damn use to me," I say, still trying to diagnose the way Betterwheatling stands talking to me; he avoids my eye, refrains from looking at his watch, but not in impatience with me (which I can always tell the look of). Why is he wearing his coat, which is the clue, of course: Betterwheatling should be leaving for another party, but cannot because he doesn't know if I am invited or not. And here comes Cilena with her coat and William, who says for me to get mine. We're going on to the Friendlings'. Maurie and Ulla will come as soon as they turf everybody out.

Young Lucinella is digging for her coat in the mound on the bed. I avoid her eyes; I don't know if she's invited to the Friendlings' or not.

"Well," she says. "Goodbye!" She stands, giving it one moment more in which to happen.

I could invite her to the Friendlings' with William and me.

She says, "Well. Goodbye!"

"Goodbye," I say. "Come back in ten years and we'll talk."

On the way to the Friendlings', William, who is high, gets pesty and keeps saying *why* won't I marry him.

"I probably will," I say.

"You don't *love* me," he whines and, craning his neck into a U like Chagall's birthday lover, sticks his outraged face into mine.

"I do," I say, "I love you." It's probably true. It's just that there must be more to love than love.

We dump our coats on the mound on the Friendlings' bed.

Winterneet comes out of the john, sees William, and says, "I meant to drop you a line to tell you how much I admire your Margery Kempe." William's eyes cross. Winterneet is thoughtful. "Nobody has used the ballad form so well in a while," he says, and walks into the Friendlings' living room.

"I thought his bit was not to remember who you are?" I say.

"That was at another party," says William. Unsnubbed, he looks amused and charming.

Benjamin walks toward me through the crowd.

"Saul Mailer is supposed to be here. Why does one *come* to these wretched things?" he asks and his eyes quicken in recognition even as I have that déjà-vu feeling of déjà vu as I answer, "In case it is the right one."

Will is bringing me a drink and says, "Saul Mailer is here!" And, really, there, in a little clearing of homage, aging, with a small pot, graying, curly, rather beautiful, stands Saul Mailer, talking to a furiously pretty girl.

I refuse to add my attention and turn my back. Now my back gives him my attention.

Will says he saw a sign in the Uffizi translated into funny English, listing the reasons why visitors are not to touch the famous paintings: "It is bad for the paint. It costs a fine"; finally, "It is useless."

Compared with Saul Mailer, Winterneet is merely eminent, but I touch his sleeve and tell him about the sign about not touching famous paintings.

Winterneet's eyes cross. He can't handle my mentioning fame to his face and says, "I don't know what you mean."

"Yes, you do," I say. Winterneet looks startled. "We think fame has one foot in the millennium, and want to connect ourselves."

"Nonsense," says Winterneet, looking to right and left, beginning to walk off, but I keep beside him. "I *know* it's nonsense!" I say, craning my neck into a U to oblige him to look me in the eye. "That's what I *mean*, Winterneet. Finally it's useless!"

Winterneet says he is going to freshen up his drink.

Where's William?

William is talking with Saul Mailer. I walk over and stick my nose into the space between them.

William is pretending not to see me because he's in the middle of his story about the miracle at sea when God stops only Margery of all the company of pilgrims from throwing up by whispering in her ear: "Keep your head down and don't look at the waves."

I turn ninety degrees right and smile at Newman. He says, "Fra hog higo na mo."

I say, "Fra hog na mo pen." He frowns. What have I said!

"Fra hog me," he says, and adds he is surprised I would fall into that particular and, if he may say, not uncommon liberal fallacy, and walks away.

I perform a left quarter turn, but there's nobody there.

No one on my right. I look into my bucket. It is empty. I am ashamed. Where is William?

There's Newman, on the sofa, talking into Ulla's open mouth.

By the bar Maurie stands with the furiously pretty girl.

Meyers and Winterneet are talking in the corner.

Frank and Alice Friendling and Cilena are laughing.

Betterwheatling, who would be so much easier to love, is wearing his overcoat.

"Saul Mailer is here," I tell him. He says he knows.

"Are you leaving?" I ask.

He says the Bernards are having people over for Harry's birthday. "Cilena, let's go."

Betterwheatling and Cilena have gone.

Now it's Friendling sitting on the sofa with Ulla, who seems about to swallow him.

"Have you seen William?" I ask them.

"Try the bedroom," Ulla says.

In the bedroom mirror I watch Meyers hunting for his coat on the bed; by tacit covenant sealed in the silence on Maurie's sofa, I do not turn and he tiptoes out behind my back.

There's no one in the bathroom.

In the foyer Benjamin is laughing with the furiously pretty girl.

There's a man in the kitchen making coffee. He turns. It's Saul Mailer.

"Have you seen William?" I ask him,

"Have you tried the dining room?" he asks. "There's an impressive pâté from Zabar's. Coffee?" he suggests. His aggressively blue eyes smile into mine, and that does it. I want to go home!

William is eating pâté.

"Let's go home," I say.

"Now? When it's beginning to be fun?"

"I'm drunk and sleepy and about to cry."

"Eat something," says William. He feeds me a marinated mushroom.

"William! The Bernards are having people over and didn't invite us." I drop a tear.

"Who are the Bernards?" asks William.

"I don't know. They don't even know us and already they've decided we're not charming or interesting enough to invite to Harry's birthday."

"*I* think you are charming and interesting," says William.

"Because you love me. That's like one's mother saying it and doesn't prove a thing."

"J. D. Winterneet thinks you're very bright," says William.

"He doesn't love me!" I cry.

"Ulla says you're looking fabulous."

"But, William, she says that to all of us so we'll forgive her being beautiful. You know Dylan Thomas's twosome, 'Always one, pert and pretty, and always one with glasses.' That's Ulla and me, since high school, and so I became a poet."

"Maurie is publishing your poems," says William.

"It's no use, William. Praise doesn't feed into the part of me that's hungry. The two systems don't interconnect. A mistake in the plumbing. Why do you take my hand out of your pocket?"

"It tickles," says William.

But I shake my head. "At Maurie's you took my hand off your arm and walked away."

William wipes my tears with his handkerchief. "You can put your hand in my pocket," he says. "You can tickle me any time. Have a mushroom."

"It's not only my hand," I say. "Remember the little servant girl in the Chekhov story? She runs errands all day long, and at night she has to rock the baby so the mistress can sleep, and in the morning, while she's cleaning the master's boot, she yearns to crawl into the darkness of the shaft and sleep."

"You can crawl in," says William, feeding me mushrooms. The room distends at the headlong speed with which I diminish. William picks me up and puts me in his pocket.

"I've thought of a joke," I say, poking out my head.

"What?" he says.

"What do you do if the Great Orgasm doesn't bring on the millennium?"

"What?" he says.

"Wait till the Second Coming."

"Go to sleep," says William.

And now, on their giant legs, Maurie and Ulla, the Friendlings, Saul Mailer, and Newman, and J. D. Winterneet, and Benjamin with the furiously pretty girl are coming to the feast.

Before I curl up to sleep, I fold my hands neatly. "Forgive me my vanities as I forgive all of you yours."

"What's the matter, Lucinella?"

"It's 'The Bucket,' William! It doesn't matter! Nobody will read it and they're right. Even I don't particularly want to read it."

"Poor Lucinella!" says William, "and you've worked so long and so hard."

"My working confers no obligation on the reader."

"Poor darling," says William, who saw me through that first, tentative skeleton plan, underlined with green, blue, and orange felt tip. For months William watched me sharpen my twelve pencils down to nubbins. Then, on that February night, at Maurie's, while I was chatting with Betterwheatling, my Underground dovetailed with my Bucket and I was struck as with the shock of coincidence, by which the people whom I kept telling and telling it kept failing to be struck, because it wasn't their, it was *my*, coincidence of two disparate ideas that explained everything. Rightness ramified down to the least of my metaphors, which I cross-referenced with my meanings on five-by-three index cards. I kept shuffling and by midsummer I'd realigned the skeleton correctly and recognized the creature. Last night my end collided with my beginning. This morning I woke and saw that the whole thing *doesn't matter!*

I call Ulla on the telephone to tell her I've written a poem that doesn't matter.

"Read it to me," she says. Ulla is really a good friend.

Ulla says both in conception and execution this is the best thing I have ever done.

"But, Ulla," I say, "what about the contradiction in the second stanza?"

"That's what I mean," Ulla says. "You have knotted the first and third stanzas across the denial of both in the second, creating an incredibly subtle model of our broken modern processes."

What's seductive about Ulla's enthusiasm is she's so specific. "It is the inevitable sequel," she says, "to your 'Root Cellar.'" She recites my poem in its entirety, correctly emphasized. I want to marry Ulla.

"But," I say. I tell her whence I plagiarized the opening idea. "Exactly," she says, "you have used those resonances in your own vastly richer context."

I experience a sensation like squinching up against more than I can accommodate of something that is forcing in upon me, and try my last line of defense. "What about the half-assed banality of the last line, Ulla?"

Ulla explicates exactly the depths I had intended.

Why do I experience her going on to say she's read nothing quite like it in Western literature as an act of hostility on Ulla's part?

"What's the matter, Lucinella?"

"It's this soap opera I'm writing. It's a story, about people. Horrible!"

"Why write it then?" asks William.

"To have something to read. Everybody likes soap opera. I myself read it all the time. I like stories."

"What about your poems? They're good."

"I know they are," I say, "but I never read them. Nobody does except my soap-opera heroine, who's a poetry reader, poor thing. Such a lot of trouble!"

"What seems to be the matter?'

"Just that her latest catastrophe is running out its course to the inevitable resolution. If I don't hurry, she'll make it into bed with the man she loves. I've known all along that I should be planting the seeds of a new disaster, but I'm no good at plotting. What I love is to get right down to the excruciations."

"What is your soap opera called?"

"*Forever Tomorrow.*"

"What's it about?"

"Bliss and disaster in their most exquisite forms. The Great Orgasm held indefinitely in abeyance, and doom perpetually, barely avoided. The trouble is I'm fresh out of calamities. Five hundred years of fiction have exhausted our resources."

"For instance," says my straight man.

"Depending on the style and preoccupation of the age, there was evil pure, in the guise of a witch or devil, or the machinations by elements at court for selfish purposes. Then there's fate: the inherited enmity of the two lovers' families, an abnormal length of nose. There used to be moral compunctions: nine hundred pages of chastity preserved against all odds, or the bonds of fealty, or a prior marriage to a crazy lady imprisoned in an upstairs room, or tyrannical fathers implementing the taboos of class to keep our lovers apart. Or one can separate their actual bodies by means of a naked sword in the bed or geographical distance due to war, from which the lover returns decades too late, or with a permanently damaged member, or suffering hysterical amnesia, paralysis, or blindness. There's the temporary insanity of one or the other in alternation, simple games of lovers' leapfrog, or with Midsummer-Night complications. There's always the misunderstanding that can be perpetuated by withholding the communication that would explain it.

"Finally there's the psychological foul-up. My heroine's problem was the gap between her arrogance and her abjection, which a successful analysis will resolve within the next six or seven pages, but I know what I can do. I'll make the syndicate kidnap them and lock *him* in an abandoned warehouse and *her* in a vault, no, an icehouse—which hasn't been done this season. Don't talk to me, William."

I have resumed writing.

"William, what's the matter?"

"My poem is no good," says William.

"Yes, it is," I say. "William, you're wrong. Your poem is very good. It's very funny."

"You and I, Lucinella," William says, "know that my poetry is worthless."

"Poor William," I say. "That's terrible!"

"Maybe I'm wrong," cries William. "Maybe it's that my poetry is so original, so unlike anything to which it could be compared, that I myself might hardly understand how really good my poem is, do you think? Lucinella? Do you love me?"

"Yes."

(I do? I *don't*? I did, I remember, just now, before he asked me if I did, but right this moment I don't remember what love feels like.)

"Will you marry me?" asks William.

"Yes," I say, and my heart falls on the ground.

Ulla calls me on the telephone. *The Magazine*, in collaboration with an upstate university, is sponsoring a symposium and Maurie wants me to be the woman poet. "A weekend in May in the country!" says Ulla. "Everybody's coming, except Alice. Friendling has left her—you didn't know?"

"No!" I cry. I like Alice. Why am I smiling?

"And Meyers," says Ulla, "if he recovers from his nervous breakdown."

"What happened!" I cry, appalled. I'm grinning.

"It was at our place," Ulla says. "We were sitting on the sofa. I was explaining his profound influence on my writing, when he went into a psychotic episode. Winterneet is doing all right after his heart attack."

"I had no idea!" I have begun to giggle.

"They put old Lucinella in a home," says Ulla, "suffering from aphasia."

When we stop laughing, Ulla asks, "So. How is it being married to William?"

"I'm thinking of leaving him."

"We're bringing young Lucinella," says Ulla. "She's got a crush on Maurie. It will be good for her to see him coming to breakfast in his crumpled pajamas showing a white hairy triangle of belly the fly doesn't close.

And so she washed the soot off her face and hands, opened the walnut, and took out the dress that shone like the sun.

Grimm

Young Lucinella takes the bus downtown to look for a new housecoat. It isn't that there's anything the matter with her old one, except it's not the kind in which to come down the stairs to breakfast.

On the rack, in the lingerie department, robes handwoven of Thai silk glow with the self-generated ruby, cerulean, amber, and natural light of the raw yarn. The outlandishness of price adds a magnificence young Lucinella can in no way afford, so she might as well try on the red one, please. The saleslady genuinely stares. "It does something for you!" she says, and young Lucinella, too, sees herself suddenly lovely, lips parted in surprise, eyes rapt, her skin glamorous in the reflected pink luster. "It isn't me," she says. She buys the housecoat in the no-color of raw sacking.

Young Lucinella takes the elevator down to the stationery department, remembering that she needs a notebook for the brand-new poem she is going to write, and goes home and puts the new notebook in a fresh white folder.

V

They've put us in a fine old fraternity on campus. I unpack and come down the stairs. There are voices. I open a door into a kitchen. At a large deal table Ulla and Cilena Betterwheatling are making sandwiches for lunch. "Lucinella!" cries Ulla. "Come in! You can make the mayonnaise and help us gossip. Why did the Friendlings get divorced?" The emotions we imagine excite us. Like children mucking in the warm, delicious mud, we mold the Friendlings' disaster into hypotheses.

"Shush, *please*," Maurie says.

"Why don't you use the hall phone?" Ulla asks.

"Because I like to be where everybody else is," Maurie says.

"Why did one get married?" Ulla asks. She stands still, holding a green pepper, Cilena arrests her knife, I stop whipping. Three wives in our bare arms and summer skins, trying to remember love.

"A symposium on writing," Maurie explains, into the

telephone. "Hell no—a short opening statement—couple of sentences. Lucinella, our token woman, will talk about 'Why Write?' The Zeuses are flying in tonight. He'll be our writer from outside New York and his subject is 'Why a Symposium?' "

"Why can't *I* be in the damn symposium?" asks William, who is making Bloody Marys.

"Because," says Maurie, "we have J. D. Winterneet to be our elder, and Meyers our younger, poet." Into the telephone he says, "Meyers's subject is 'Why Read?' I'll take 'Why Publish?' and Pavlovenka is doing her usual comedy routine, 'Why Teach Writing?' Afterward we'll have ourselves one hell of a party. Terrific! Great!" Maurie hangs up. "Newman is coming, so that's our black, and this year they're not even asking to be in on things."

Ulla says, "Maurie, don't pick! Go slice your own pepper. Try the red one, it's sweet," she says and feeds him a piece and now I remember why one wanted to be married and have someone always around to be fantastically nice to, but not William, exactly.

We sit around the table, eat, drink, and talk. My theory is Frank Friendling woke one day, discovered he was forty, happy in his work, his friends, and in love with his handsome, intelligent wife, and still he was nothing but Frank Friendling and he couldn't bear it.

William thinks it's the claustrophobia of marriage.

Cilena says it's boredom.

No, Ulla says, it's the hostility. She hands Maurie a knife and a carrot, and says, "Scrape. We're making navarin for sixteen people. I will start cutting up the meat."

"*I'll* cut up," says Maurie.

"Cut it out, Maurie!" Ulla says.

"I'll cut the capers," says Maurie.

"I'll make another batch of Marys," William says.

"I'll make the jokes," says Maurie.

"While everybody else is working!" shouts Ulla.

"Dear," says Maurie, "that's my joke you're stepping on." Sharply, briefly, they quarrel.

Betterwheatling comes in—how can he work when we are having so much fun down here—and Meyers fetches himself a sandwich to take back upstairs.

"Okay, okay," says Maurie, "so I'll make my special apple charlotte, if somebody will peel the apples."

"I will." It's J. D. Winterneet in the doorway. Pavlovenka drove him down. All afternoon we sit around the table, cook together, talk; we laugh a lot; once in a while the house gives itself a shake: like pieces in a kaleidoscope we're rearranged. Ulla asks Maurie for the car keys to go and fetch old Lucinella from the station. Meyers comes back. He can't write anything at all in this rotten house. Now Pavlovenka leaves to unpack and Winterneet must take his nap after the long ride. Betterwheatling, who stands behind me, says he's got to put in an hour on the galleys of his book.

Don't everybody go away!

"Betterwheatling," I ask (I've had a lot of Marys), "so what *do you* do when marriage palls?"

"I suffer," Betterwheatling says, surprised.

By five everyone's come down. William is making the martinis. Maybe a commune is the right idea after all.

By six, happy, and in love with everybody, I go up to take a nap.

At a point in time William touches me on the shoulder.

"*What?*"

"Dinner, Lucinella," he says, but I'm out for the night.

Another point in time: the mattress dips. William has sat down on the bed. The bed rocks. William is taking his shoes and socks off.

"What's happening? Where's everybody?"

"It's past two o'clock. You go back to sleep."

But I have sat straight up. "What have you all been doing? What's going on down there?"

"Nothing, Lucinella. Maurie is reading a manuscript. Ulla and Meyers went for a midnight walk. The Zeuses' plane was late—Jesus, is she beautiful! A Renoir woman sculpted by Michelangelo. Young Lucinella did a double take."

"Because that's what she would look like if they'd given her a choice. And Zeus?"

"As always, two heads taller than everybody else, but now that he's past middle age, I forgive him. I'm drunk," says William, rolling into bed. He puts his arms around me.

"What, Will, what is it, love?"

William muffles his weeping at the base of my throat, and mumbles that he cannot stand it, he cannot, cannot, cannot, cannot stand it.

"What, what, sweet?" I murmur.

"Being married to you!" William wails.

"The nagging, is it?" I ask him.

"That. But not only that! Think of all the other women I can never, never, never marry now!"

"Poor darling, my poor love." I kiss his forehead. "With me, it's not so much wanting to marry everybody else. It's that it isn't you, exactly, I wanted to be married to."

"Poor sweet," William says, and kisses my throat over and over.

"I once wrote a poem," I murmur into William's hair, "called 'The Best Seat,' about this woman who goes to the theater and can't afford a good seat, or there is none available, probably both. First she moves two rows forward, then looks for an empty place farther center. She genuinely suffers because she doesn't have the best seat in the house. Of course she misses the performance."

"And now imagine it's the *only* performance there is going to be!" William is howling with pain.

"Shush, William, shhh."

I'm wide awake. I study the sleeping man's flesh, purple in the darkness, and find it in my heart to wish William dead. How dare he not love me all, not want me only! My instep tickles. I inch myself out of the constriction of William's arms, pull the sheet up to cover his naked shoulder, and softly close the door behind me.

I meet Meyers coming up the stairs.

"Morning, Meyers," I say.

"Good night," says Meyers.

In the living room, Maurie is snoring on the sofa under a green afghan. A manuscript rises and falls on his belly.

I look into the kitchen, where Betterwheatling is correcting galleys at the great deal table. He looks up.

"What's so funny?" he asks, because I sit down and laugh and laugh and laugh. "It's this house," I say. "Everywhere somebody is writing something, or eating something . . . or sleeping or just getting up or just turning in." Betterwheatling yawns, aligns the edges of his papers, and stands up. "Two A.M. and tomorrow the silly symposium! Good night."

"Good morning, Lucinella!" say Zeus and Hera. They're in their pajamas. "Good to see you," says Zeus. His basso profundo is self-accompanied by a diapason one octave lower. He's hugging me to his colossal chest; my forehead prickles with his primeval beard, so different from the ever-changing decorations that grow on the faces of my New York friends. And Hera! Oh, those great, ageless, round, blond forms . . .

"We flew in late and missed dinner," she says.

"I overslept it."

We look in the icebox. Hera warms up the leftover

navarin. I make coffee. Zeus has discovered the drawer where they keep the knives and forks. We three old friends sit together around the table.

"Who was it told me you turned down the presidency of—what's the name of that college in upstate New York? Olympia? Ha, ha. I'm sorry," I say and blush.

"That's quite all right," Zeus says. "One of the liabilities of my situation. The irresistible, goddamn jokes."

"His students gave him a lightning-shaped silver tie pin. Ha ha," Hera says.

"I find I like teaching," Zeus says, "but no more politics! And I want to do my book."

"What are you writing?" I ask.

"The longest history in history," says Hera. "Open at both ends."

"Right now," Zeus says eagerly, "I'm working on the chapter about what Professor Preuss so charmingly called man's *Ur-dummheit* or 'primal stupidity,' such as the cult of Zeus Meilichios, worshipped in the form of an enormous bearded snake, attended by a small pet man . . . " I am watching Hera watching the enormous male across the table with that wifely look, one part anxiety, two parts exasperation, but I can tell she cares for him. I'm jealous of that embattled, ancient intimacy.

"You heard about the Friendlings?" I ask them. And I tell them about William and me. "I really admire the Betterwheatlings, and couples like the Winterneets, and you. You've survived claustrophobia, mutual boredom, chronic hostilities—whatever! There's something profoundly respectable, something truly romantic about old marriages," I wind up breathless with enthusiasm.

"Well, well, well, well, well," says Hera, giving me a look. "Well, well, let's not get carried away. *I'm* going back to bed," she says. "Good night."

"But really," I say, "can you, Zeus, from the man's point of view, explain to me why Friendling would walk out on Alice, who's a smart, funny, good-looking, and bloody nice woman?"

"Why indeed!" says Zeus. "Why don't we shape up and fuck the perfectly splendid persons right in our own beds?"

Why are Zeus and I sitting in our pajamas talking about marriage and sex while the night turns from black to a sharp electric blue to a dead gray to rose to gold outside the kitchen window?

For young Lucinella, in her room at the head of the stairs, getting dressed is an intellectual act and her new housecoat the statement of an aesthetic principle undermined by another side of a different argument. Its silk being pure is a virtue sine qua non—young Lucinella would never wear any artificial put-on—but its being silk, and for breakfast, embarrasses her. Moreover, she has cut the phony golden button off and hasn't found an honest one to keep her held together.

In her despair young Lucinella leans her head into her hands and smiles. She laughs out loud as her dilemma shapes itself into an anecdote. She needs someone to tell it to.

Young Lucinella comes down the stairs holding the front edges of her housecoat in a fist to cover her bosom. She stands in the kitchen door. "Does anyone have a pin or a piece of string?"

"Good morning, Lucinella," Zeus and I say.

"How did you know it's me?" she mumbles.

"What?" Zeus inclines his head.

"What's the use of my new housecoat?" says young Lucinella, who exposes the comic turns she discovers in her mind the way a prettier flirt flashes a knee or unbuttons a breast, with the same shy, brave hope of connecting her eyes with another's, preferably male, if not, mine will do, and in case neither of us is going to return her smile (in which case she hopes we will be so good as not to notice she has offered it) she bends to pick up the passing college cat and hides her long nose in its fur. She presses a passionate cheek against the fiercely struggling body, which bends into a U and bites her on the nose.

"Look at the time!" I say.

"You're leaving?" cries young Lucinella, and rises too. She dumps the cat.

"I have to go and write my opening statement for the symposium tonight."

"Don't you want breakfast?" Zeus asks young Lucinella, who raises her eyes to where his eyes are looking pleasantly at her, and flees up the stairs close on my heels.

It's noon. I'm done. Where's William? Where *is* everybody? I can hear Meyers's typewriter still going.

Downstairs, the windows stand wide. A breeze brushes my bare arms. I put my head out of the front door. The porch is empty. Sunlight. Lilac in bloom! A young rabbit sits on the lawn, so close I can see the nose waffling. I hold still, afraid my heart knocking in my chest, the faint presence of voices I can now perceive in the house behind me, might scare him off, but the rabbit sits. They must work on a different system. My nerves are already fidgeting, my hand inching toward the book someone's left on that chair. Who's reading Wordsworth? Wouldn't *he* scoff if I opened to a page, while nature is blessing me with one of her babies at such close quarters, sitting as still as stone for me to watch. Or *is* it . . . it's a little stone rabbit! With waffling nose!

How long is that rabbit going to go on sitting there like that? Shoo, rabbit, I think. Brrrr. Pssst!

The rabbit goes on sitting. I creep guiltily back inside the house to see who it is in the living room.

It's William, cross-legged on the carpet in front of young Lucinella, who sits with her left buttock on the edge of the sofa, her right leg poised, so as to have been about to leave at a first sign that she bores her companion, for which the acute point of her intelligence is ever on the alert. She listens anxiously to what he's saying, afraid of finding him a bore.

William is saying, "When Margery gets back to England, her confessor says he hears she's brought a baby home from the Holy Land, and Margery answers—listen to this—she says, 'Sir, this same child God hath sent me, I have brought him.' "

"Meaning?" asks young Lucinella, moving forward, to the edge of excitement.

"Exactly!" says William.

"Hi!" I say loudly from the doorway.

"Hi," says young Lucinella.

"Hi," William says. "It means either, 'The only one I have had anything to do with is God, so how can I have brought home a baby?' "

"Or?" says young Lucinella, her eyes shining as if she were about to weep.

"Or," William says, "'The only one I've had anything to do with is God, so it's his baby.'"

Young Lucinella slips down to the carpet beside William. I slip out into the foyer and I know the precise point where the first sharp crystals of the new ice age are forming, right here, in my belly.

Hera is drinking her coffee upstairs on the veranda.

"Tell me a story," I beg her. "How did you and Zeus meet?"

"We're closely related, you remember," says Hera. "For eons he chased me, and I ran, until he turned himself into a cuckoo, so wet and bedraggled I nestled him between my breasts. The wedding night," says Hera, "lasted three hundred years."

"William and young Lucinella come out on the front porch below us. I lean over the railing and watch William crush a leaf of lilac and hold his finger under young Lucinella's nose. She draws her head back. They saunter together and disappear around the left corner of the house. "How does one handle jealousy?" I cry.

"Badly," says Hera. "You know the story of Zeus and Semele, how I went to her disguised as a neighbor and whispered, 'Next time tell him to show himself in his true nature or deny him your bed!' Zeus, of course, came in thunder and lightning. That was the end of *her*. Poor Io! They thought it was Zeus who turned her into a cow and sent a gadfly after her, but it was me! And it wasn't only jealousy," says Hera. "Nobody knows that all the time I was watching my husband chasing every skirt and saw the skirts running, and knew he wasn't going to make them except in some fool disguise, though everybody thinks it was to fool me."

"Why did they run? I mean, I really like Zeus," I say, and blush.

"I know you do," says Hera and gives me that look I don't understand. "Maybe," she says, "he wasn't all the prize you think."

"Because of the skirts? All those nymphs and princesses?"

"All those princesses, and not only that," says Hera. "It was the brutality, the cowardice."

"Zeus's cowardice?" I don't like that.

"Cowardice, yes," she says. "You remember how his mother—Earth, you know—prophesied the child that Metis bore was going to dethrone him. Damned if Zeus, like his father and grandfather before him, doesn't open up his mouth and with one gulp . . . and not the child only!

Mother and all. So now *he* had to birth the baby. Have you ever been around a man who's got a cold in the head? Imagine Zeus with Pallas Athene ready to spring from his brow! Then there was the time Typhon stormed Olympus when Zeus didn't happen to have his thunder on him. What does he do but turn himself into a ram and skidaddle to save his own skin! When the monster made a pass at me, don't you think Zeus strung *me* from the rafters of heavens with an anvil tied to each ankle—though he *said* it was in punishment for my rebellion. Ares had to come and get me down." Hera sits very straight, chin high, still smoldering. She has forgotten not a tittle of her husband's ancient offenses.

We are silent. "So why do we stick with them!" I say.

"Oh," Hera says, "because one's tied to them by one's own possessiveness, by sex, I suppose. Not so much now any more, but I used, once in a while, to borrow Aphrodite's girdle . . . And by pity."

"Pity for Zeus?"

"Oh yes," Hera says. "It's watching the erosion of their powers that breaks the heart and grapples you to them even when they no longer want you. You've read your Aeschylus?"

"Well . . . " I say.

"Read it," says Hera. "Read where the buccaneer god and philanderer has a stature second hardly to Jehovah, before Euripides began to psychologize and Plato turned us into literature. The Romans carved two frown lines between Zeus's eyes, set his heads on prefabricated torsos, and disseminated him through the known world. In the Christian era, he had to go underground, and when he turns up again, he's gone baroque, going rococo. By the eighteenth century what is he except a self-conscious grace note of erudition? Yesterday I saw him in company with Thor and Green Lantern, if you please—not all badly drawn—in a kiddie comic. Tomorrow he will find himself a minor character in some Tom, Dick, or Harry's comical new novel. Desecrated, deposed, exiled, but incapable of dying, no longer god and unwilling—or is it unable?—to be human, what can he do but turn into an intellectual, write a book, research his own descent—heaven forgive me, maybe it's an ascent—from a bearded snake to what? A refugee college professor!"

"Lucinella!"

It's William calling me. "I'm coming!" I cry.

Before the symposium we huddle in the kitchen as if by prearrangement. Maurie is having himself a small, stiff whiskey. "I feel euphoric," I tell everybody. "What am I feeling so euphoric for?" I ask Meyers, who looks stoned on neat terror.

Betterwheatling is sweating. I have an idea for a poem about the physical despair of a fat man inside too many layers of cloth, but Ulla, who is passing, says, "Betterwheatling, take your jacket off." No wonder everybody wants to marry Ulla.

William brings me a drink. "I'm fine," I keep saying. "I'm positively euphoric."

William says, "If I go like this, it means 'Nobody can hear you,' and like this means 'Slow down.'"

"I'll be fine," I say. "You won't remember me," I say to Newman, who looks fabulous in flannels and a ribbed navy turtleneck. "We met at Maurie's."

"And you told me your theory about parties," he says.

"And you told me yours about power, which I didn't understand but I knew it was fascinating. And the second time that same evening we meet at the Friendlings' and you snapped my head off."

Newman jumps. "I did?" he says and takes my arm. "I did not!"

"Okay, okay, okay," says Maurie. "Everybody. Let's get this show on the road. Who has a car?"

"I'll drive Lucinella," says Newman, and takes my elbow.

"William, you take young Lucinella and Meyers. Pavlovenka is driving J. D. Winterneet. Betterwheatling and Cilena, will you please take old Lucinella."

Cilena says, "The three of us can sit up front if Betterwheatling would either wear his jacket or throw the damn thing in the back. This silly symposium is bad for the temper. Are you all right there in the middle?" she asks old Lucinella.

Betterwheatling is manipulating key and shift. Old Lucinella stares in surprise at the fat forearm moving a quarter inch from hers: it has bulk, gives off a warmth; old Lucinella can barely believe what she is remembering.

She says, "Why *are* we having this damn silly symphony . . . sympathy . . . I mean . . . " She shakes her head, squinches up her eyes, and stares where the missing word keeps just out of sight.

"There's Maurie!" Betterwheatling says. "I'll let you two off here."

"That happens more and more these days," old Lucinella says. "I've got a case of galloping aphorism . . . aphrodisiac . . . " She laughs and shakes her head. "Aphids . . . " She shakes her head. "What's the aph I'm after?" she asks Cilena, who's holding the door to the auditorium for her. Cilena inclines her head and asks, "What?"

Old Lucinella laughs and shakes her head.

VI

Already Maurie is chivying us up the steps and out into the merciless illumination of the platform.

"We might have a couple of lights in the auditorium, so we can see whom we are talking at," he says to the student, a tall black kid, who is stagemanaging the water pitcher and glasses on the narrow speakers' table that runs the width of the stage.

"Betterwheatling, kindly take this end. Zeus, please . . . Lucinella, next to Zeus. Meyers . . . "

(Meyers's eyelids are neon-pink. Now he has nothing to hold on to except his own extravagantly drooping blond mustache.)

"I'll sit next to Meyers," says Maurie. "Then Newman, please."

(When did he change into that satin blouse, open to the navel, showing a silver fist on a heavy chain around his throat?)

"Then Winterneet."

(And when did he diminish? His bank teller's navy suit I remember from that first time at Yaddo hangs in elephant folds.)

"Pavlovenka, if you don't mind taking the other end?"

(Pavlovenka, wearing red-and-white-and-blue-striped stockings, doesn't mind. Her beautiful, fat face glows.)

Where's William sitting in this solid blackness in front of us? Where is young Lucinella? And Ulla, and the rest of our crowd?

Now Maurie is welcoming the audience to this symposium on writing. Zeus is going to get the ball rolling.

Zeus rises, enormous at my side. He says the word "symposium" comes from the Greek *syn* ("together") and *pinein* ("to drink") and still connotes just such a meeting of old friends as are here come together on this platform, for a free flowing of ideas . . .

"And now a few words from Lucinella. Her subject is 'Why Write?' " Maurie says, and already my voice is launched upon the depth of this silence, and there's no hope of a reprieve ex machina, now I have got to go on reading all the way down to the bottom of the page. I feel my words rolling in my mouth. Fondly I raise my eyes to the audience inside the darkness before me. How nice of all those grownups to sit so quietly, listening to me! Zeus and Meyers laugh; everybody's laughing. I guess I made a joke, it's just that I can't remember what it's all about, this writing I am reading, nor is there any way now to stop and make it out. But I'm a pro. I carry on with this unlovable and strange new stridency—where was I when this authoritative note was creeping into my voice? So this is the world's expertise! Me! And it's true; I do know what I mean when I say, "Writing is like brushing my teeth, without which the day is misspent, I quarrel with the grocer, will get no letter from a friend, and mislay my key, so there's no way for god to get into his heaven," I wind up emphatically. Already? Over so soon!

Zeus smiles at me.

Maurie is introducing Meyers. I look anxiously toward him.

Meyers says, "There's a character in a Huxley novel who arranges his suicide for the moment before his friends are due to arrive. Instead of a note, they find Beethoven's last quartet revolving on the phonograph. If that doesn't explain, nothing can. My subject tonight is 'Why Read Poetry?' and I'll explain by reading you a poem." Meyers inclines his head to listen to himself.

Through that pure virgin shrine,
That sacred veil drawn o'er Thy glorious noon,
That men might look and live, as glowworms shine . . .

Newman blows his nose into his handkerchief.

Maurie passes me a sheet of paper on which it says: "What's with the auditorium lights?"

I look toward the stage manager, hovering in the wings, and wiggle a finger for his attention, point up at the lights and out into the auditorium, but he doesn't understand. He's disappeared. I look toward Maurie. He signals: Do something.

I push my chair noiselessly back. I feel adventurous, walking into the wings. There is the bank of switches; the top row is marked "Auditorium." I feel efficient.

"Don't do that," says the stage manager out of the shadows.

"What! Why?" I say. "It's just we want more of a sense of colloquy. We want to see who's out there."

"Oh no, you don't," he says. "That's what you *don't* want to see."

Is this some gothic scene I've got myself involved in? I don't believe this! The kid and I are staring at each other. He is large, and black. I go back to my seat out on the platform, avoiding Maurie's eyes. Winterneet and Pavlovenka seem to be scrapping.

"I tell my students," she's saying, " to write what they feel, to experiment, to throw off the tyrannical old forms."

(Hear, hear, I think.)

"And impose on the poor young people the tyranny of freedom?" says Winterneet.

(Hear, hear, I think again.)

Pavlovenka worries. She doesn't like people saying unkind things about freedom. "How d'you mean, 'tyranny'?"

"I mean it's hard having to invent a free-verse form for every new occasion."

"It isn't hard for *my* students to write free verse," Pavlovenka says.

"But mayn't it be hard," says Winterneet—his pale nose pinched, eyes gummed by his recent illness, he turns his famous, bald, old head with weary sweetness in Pavlovenka's direction—"might it not be hard, forgive me, on their readers? Even the often dazzling experiments in *The Magazine*"— here he turns toward Maurie—"seem to be *choosing* to be opaque and boring."

Maurie, who seemed to be dozing in his chair, rouses himself to say, "Which brings me to my subject: 'Why Publish What Nobody Will Read?' The reading public, not to speak of the publishing community, is a bunch of Gertrudes. Poor Gertrude! She's so horrified to see the Prince familiarly in conversation with what looks to her exactly like the empty air, she *must* conclude he's mad or, at best, a put-on artist. Remember the little man who slashed the early Picasso canvases? One concluded *he* was mad—why this passion? Why not stay quietly at home? But how *could* he ignore what must be proved to be nothing, or prove him blind—and deaf, and dumb! That's very, very terrible! No wonder these Gertrudes plant the letter for our execution in our pockets and put us out to sea."

"And while you," says Newman, "are communing with your elitist ghost, the real world burns."

The speakers along the table stir. Newman, overwrought and intense, leans toward Maurie, who leans back in his chair like some fat Farouk of the intellect, and says, "Yes." His smile is warm and his eyes are spunky.

But Newman will not let Maurie be charming. He bends his neck into a U and forces Maurie to face what he is about to say and says, "I'm talking about hunger."

(That's true, I think, dazzled by the enormity he means.)

"I publish poetry. The world—starves." Maurie gives the word its fullest and slowest weight. "Neither causes, nor prevents, the other."

(And that's true too, I think.)

"What you publish," says Newman, "is an elitist magazine."

"Hear, hear!" says Pavlovenka.

"Written," says Newman, "by a couple of dozen literati—"

"Of whom you are one!" says Maurie.

"—read not even by each other," says Newman.

"*I* never read it!" Pavlovenka assures him.

"I publish literature," says Maurie.

"Literature is elitist," Newman says.

"Right on," from the stage manager in the wings.

"Oh, but," Pavlovenka says.

"*What!*" Winterneet and Meyers cry.

(Is that true, I wonder.)

"Aren't you—" begins Betterwheatling.

"Errant crap," says Maurie, "and you know it, Newman."

"While Winterneet," says Newman, "is embalming the sonnet and the villanelle—" The stage manager laughs.

"You don't take my meaning," says Winterneet with irritable eagerness.

Zeus puts his mouth close to my ear and whispers, "You'll have to pay admission if you're going to enjoy yourself." (It's true. My head is turning form one to the other. How beautifully each is doing his own thing!)

"—and Lucinella," says Newman (I jump), "writes for her private prophylaxis, she says, the way she cleans her teeth—"

"*You* know what I meant," I cry, shocked. I thought I was on his side! He's righter, surely, than the rest of us. "I only meant that writing has grown as deep as habit—"

"Aren't you—" Betterwheatling tries again.

"What I meant"—Winterneet leans toward Newman—"is that to refuse forms perfected by the past is like having to invent the bed each time you want to go to sleep."

"Your forms," says Newman, "were created on the backs of blacks."

"And women," cries Pavlovenka.

"Aren't you confusing—" Betterwheatling says.

"I'm talking," says Winterneet, "about the mastery of technique."

"Technique is racist," says Newman. "Its purpose is to master slaves."

"I'll never master it!" Pavlovenka promises.

"Aren't you confusing the realms of poetry and politics?" says Betterwheatling, bending his neck into a U to force Newman's attention.

"Poetry *is* politics," says Newman.

"Oh yes," from the wings.

Meyers leans forward intently:

"God's silent, searching flight;
When my Lord's head was filled with dew,"

he says, but Newman sits back in his chair and laughs into the audience and says, "Not *my* lord."

" . . . and all
His locks are wet with the clear drops of night;
His still, soft call,"

sings Meyers, reaching across Maurie to touch Newman on the arm to make him listen. Newman trumpets into his handkerchief.

"His knocking time; the soul's dumb watch,
When spirits their fair kindred catch."

"What about their dark kindred!" shouts Newman and sticks his middle finger into the air.

"By technique, don't you see," says Winterneet—he looks exhausted—"I mean what has become as unconscious as the techniques of grammar."

"Grammar is racist," cries Newman, laughing.

"And sexist," I yell. I'm getting into the spirit.

"Except you need it to deny it," shouts Maurie.

"The hell you say!" Newman cries. "We will invent our own!"

"Absolutely! Newman, I agree with you!" calls Pavlovenka.

"That's your problem!" says Newman, without looking at her.

"Straight, or butchered," Betterwheatling says, "it will be English."

"English," pronounces Newman, with an excruciating clarity, "is an imperialist language, its grammar and vocabulary so perverted in the service of oppression and obfuscation it has lots its capacity for truth. English is no longer capable of poetry."

Pavlovenka splutters, Meyers howls, Betterwheatling, Maurie, and Winterneet have risen to their feet shouting what Newman cannot hear in the uproar. I'm helplessly laughing. I laugh and I laugh and I laugh. Zeus towers over all. "Have we come to exchange ideas or to shout one another down!" he thunders.

"I," cries Newman, "have come to break the whole thing up, and the time is now!" he calls to the audience. He raises his right hand in a fist while the left pushes the table so jug and glasses slide. We grab for our papers, which lift upon the updraft as the table overturns once and with a second somersault clatters over the edge of the platform.

"Don't forget the party!" cries Maurie over the hubbub. "At the old Fraternity! Everybody welcome! Is everyone okay down there? For Chris*sake*, will you put on the lights?" he yells at the stage manager, who flips the switches with an embarrassed smile at me and a shrug of his shoulders, and as the brown lights come on in the auditorium we see nobody's out there except our crowd in the second row on the right. Hera, Cilena bending to pick up—is it old Lucinella's shawl that's slipped under the seat? Ulla is coming forward to congratulate us. "You were terrific! I thought it went very well!" There's Frank Friendling—who's the girl with him? That's William's back disappearing up the aisle with young Lucinella. I jump off the stage, climb over the upended table, but by the time I've run up the aisle and out the door into the night, the car with William and young Lucinella is speeding off.

"Hop in!" "Ride, anybody?" Everybody is shouting hilariously. "Come with *us*, Lucinella!" Cilena and Betterwheatling say.

VII

Back at the house every room is lit, the party is in swing. People carrying their drinks from one room to another stop to ask, "How did it go?"

"Did you see William?" I ask everybody.

Here's Friendling—with the furiously pretty girl. Of course! We stop to chat. I mean to scowl, out of solidarity with Alice, whom I like, but the girl is so lovely, so intelligent, seems so much to like Friendling, I *like* her.

Friendling says yes, he thinks he saw William and young Lucinella carrying their drinks up the stairs.

I open the door into our bedroom. It's full of black people, perching on the bed, cross-legged on the rug. The stage manager waves to me.

"Have you seen William?" I ask Newman, who's leaning in the embrasure of the window surrounded by students. He reaches a hand around my waist and draws me into the circle. I'm pleased and I relax against his side.

A young girl with a face like Wedgwood basalt, in an Afro shaped into a two-by-two-foot topiary cube, is saying for her senior thesis she's constructing a soul syntax based not on inflected parts of speech, nor word order, nor the pitch of voice, but on rhythms which will be incomprehensible to whites.

I smile, trying to catch Newman's eye, but his head inclines with courteous eagerness toward the young speaker.

(Am I one of these Gertrudes?)

Newman says there is a small hill tribe he knows whose language used to be so rich in conjunctions it made possible varieties of loving outside our experience. There the smallest baby could play safely in the road, so that the women were free to be themselves. No one grew old, because their vocabulary had no word for ill or dead, nor for black, poor, ugly, stupid, or small, so it was not possible for them to use one another rudely, to ignore, exclude, or put each other down. Their grammar did not permit the concept "less" or "worse" until the missionaries introduced the comparative form, simultaneously banning the use of the eight full and five half gradations of the superlative which, in their near-infinity of intercombinations, had made possible a precision and multiformity of joy unknown to Western cultures. Now their loving conjunctions are all atrophied and turned into a singleness of hate that will, in good time, burn off the white pollution and return them to their black purity of tongue. Even now, they're gathering and training the bloodiest army on the continent.

"Where?" ask all the students. "What latitude is it? Do you need a passport?"

My eyes have filled with sulky tears because they won't let *me* come, I know, so the hell with them! I'd go away if Newman were not holding me around the waist. I don't want to hurt his feelings.

I'm fascinated by the complex intelligence the human touch conveys, by means of what? The temperature, the duration and distribution of pressure across the surface points of the four, say five square inches of Newman's palm are saying to a corresponding patch of my skin that he does not intend, that he disapproves, the natural warmth of his right hand. He curls it into the loose approximation of a fist and, resting the ball of his thumb above the bone of my hip, bores his middle finger into my flesh with increasing malignity until I yowl, "I'd better go find William!"

Bodies part to let me escape into the hall. No one watches me go. Their conversation closes over my head.

From inside her room old Lucinella hears me in the hallway asking Cilena if she's seen William anywhere, and old Lucinella keeps thinking that she is about to rise out of her chair and come to the door to tell me, "I saw William and young Lucinella carrying their drinks out to the verbena, I mean the verdure . . . verdigris . . . " She smiles at the posy of words; none of them has the right letters in the right order that so curiously coincides with a veronica . . . a vermifuge . . . vernissage . . . vichyssoise . . .

Old Lucinella still sits in the chair. Isn't she going to get up? Isn't she going downstairs to the party to talk with Ulla, and Betterwheatling . . . with Winterneet, whom she has known for more than half, more like two thirds of her life—who's so embattled now by his illness, his obsolescence, his old wife—who was it said Lena Winterneet drinks . . .

Old Lucinella knows that if she doesn't get up now she won't the next moment, nor at any moment after that. She's frightened. She hears the footsteps coming from the veranda, running past her door and down the stairs, and a second pair running after, hears William crying, "Lucinella!" She knows he does not mean her.

I cry, "Here I am, William!" I run down the stairs behind him and out through the front door in time to see him follow young Lucinella round the left corner of the house. “For crying out loud, William!” I yell, ashamed to see him chasing the silly girl, and as I come around the corner I see his narrow back, the familiar, callow neck, rounding the next bend. “Wil*liam!*” I cry. I know he hears me. He’s recognized the horror in my voice, knows that the ice age is encroaching on my heart, and runs faster and faster. We circle past the front door and I see how to save myself. I run more and more slowly till I hear William panting behind me. “Lucinella!!” he cries. I say, “Here I am!” Sweetness suffuses my blood like a substance that melts jealousy in retrospect. He catches up with me. The ice age, which never existed, recedes. I say, “Darling, one thing, and it’s important. Let there, please, William, always be truth, absolutely, between you and me. Promise,” I say and, for safety’s sake, pass quickly through the front door into the house.

VIII

In the curl of the banister stands Zeus having a quiet smoke. The party has got too hot and noisy for him, he says.

"Me too," I say. "I'm going up to bed." I lift my cheek for a good-night kiss. His tongue thrusts straight and deep between my lips and the world suspends its rotation. His hand inside my blouse touches, his mouth lifts out of mine, pronounces my name as if it were a foreign language: "Lucinella."

I'm looking into the same astonished roundness of eye that Europa saw the instant of her rape. Whether disguised as bull, or swan, or golden shower activity (as they call it on television—and which requires a great imaginative effort), or as my aging intellectual, your true lover has the grace to be dazzled by each new passion. His veteran confidence needs no double-entendre to make loopholes for a misunderstanding. He says, "Let's make love."

Now that I know Zeus and I are going to be lovers (and know it's him I would have wanted all along if it had occurred to me), I freeze. I want my mother! "Let's not!" I say.

"Let's," he says, waits. No rape, no suasion. There's no need.

I say, "All right," and his immense arms take me up and lift me through the front door down the steps.

"But you're married," I say, ashamed to be so vulgar, but I have been jealous. It is Hera who's my sister. What does Zeus know!

"We won't tell her," he says, on the faintest rising pitch of irritation. "Hera and I've been married these eons and have eternity to go." He carries me over the midnight fields, tree and stone, into his bed. And when the earth resumes its motion, the direction has been radically altered; I've slipped away and run back to New York. I'm not ready yet to meet him with my morning face.

At home his letter awaits me: a quick page of astonished jubilation, and what admirable prose! Happiness is its keynote.

Mine is bewilderment. I'd wanted to be virtuous—that's the prettiest dream of all!—but now elation must learn to co-exist with my guilty treachery and it's not hard—oh, shabby guilt. As for happiness, there's a word! I smile and smile, but how shall I recognize what I can't exactly remember ever meeting face to face before? And I don't know the rules. Is it all right to dispatch my prickly perplexity into Arcadia? If I could only talk with him for half an hour, I'd understand everything, and so I write him what I never meant to say: Come!

He writes back to say he will be here at 8:15 but must leave by 7:20 the next morning. He arrives on the dot.

I doubt if I'd have given Zeus a second look in his heyday, when he was gaudy with health, his dark-blue locks, his bristling beard, eyes like oxidized copper sparking pink and gold and purple lights, and his enormous size. I prefer my gods in their twilight. I lean into the voluptuous laxness of elderly flesh. Under my hands, great Zeus lies patiently; he knows how to suffer pleasure. His divine cock has lost none of its potence and his hand is omniscient.

I used to laugh at gods and kings. I'd imagined Zeus muscle-bound, stupid with power, rattling his enormous thunder, unable to control the whims and spectacular tempers of his oversized relations, but in my bed his mind moves feelingly. It's just that mine, being Jewish and from New York, leaps more nimbly, which he enjoys. I sense his smiling in the darkness. When I get silly he reaches out laughingly to fetch me home to good sense and we make love again, sleep awhile, and more love and more talking.

I ask Zeus to visit inside my head. (You are invited, too. In here he and I, and you, will get to know one another, though like every hostess I'm a little nervous. Notice how I elide my sentences and keep my book short. I'm watching for signs of a yawn burgeoning behind your compressed lips. You don't want to hurt my feelings, I know, but feel free to leave any time. Though your departing back will make a permanent dent in my confidence, one survives. I prefer it to your sufferance behind my back.)

Morning. I am chilled by the expanse of air that separates me from Zeus. He's sitting on the edge of my bed. Once he's put his socks back on, there's no seduction of mine that can keep him one minute after 7:20.

"What did I do wrong?" I ask in my letter. I think I'm joking, but Zeus, who, like me, knows how words work, hears a faint note of trouble, and finds me troublesome, and I hear the faint rising pitch of irritation in his tone. With deliberate gentleness, he maps the boundaries of our permitted pleasures, which have the circumference of points reiterated on a razor's edge. I joyfully entrust myself to his governance because I see where the two hundred and fifty-fifth, -sixth, and -seventh words of his letter are out of focus with feeling and my left nipple rises to meet the lack of Zeus's hand—why can't I recall what his hand looks like? Next time I'll study it.

I write him back a poem and all's well so long as I keep typing, but in the interval after extracting one page, before I can insert the next, desire has created the phantom of his tongue. I look down. There's nothing there—but even the reality is so palpably unlikely, always, I never believe it.

Nights, I thrust my hand into his massive absence.

I call Friendling, who's the editor of that cheapie black paperback series called Living Ancients, the ones with the skimpy margins; you have to break the spine to get at the last words of the even and first words of the odd pages. He sends me Aeschylus, Sophocles, Euripides in great empty mouthfuls of blank English verse.

I've had to stop writing my soap opera. I can't invent wanting what I've got. Even now Love sits down, here, on the edge of my bed. The mattress dips under his weight. I had forgotten the fit of his enormous chest into my arms.

This time I invite myself for a tour of the inside of Zeus's head, but keep peering at him to make sure I'm welcome; I'll retreat at a moment's notice. He's looking all around, a little surprised. He stumbles. I take him by the hand. He's used to freer movements in a larger landscape with a fresher circulation of the air, while I am most at home playing indoors, though I love to look out through other eyes, to see what the world's like when one is male, beautiful, immortal. I've never been to Greece. (Once I dreamed I sat on sand the size and shape of the map of the Isle of Naxos; my footbath was the Aegean Sea, as blue as blue, the temperature of my own blood.) I ask him what is underfoot when you stand on Olympus. How does one throw lightning? I've never been that angry. Look down, there! An aerial view of history! Imagine: to have a will capable of intervention and to refrain, though he might have sent his heroes sooner when monsters were devouring all that young flesh, but you have to look at things in their historical perspective. We know how problematical problems are compared with hindsight, and Hera never any help. Delicacy prevents speculation. I refuse to wonder what she's like to lie with (what I want to know is what it feels like to desire me), but I do ask him all about Semele, Io, and Perseus's mother—what *was* her name? I love him for the decency of his reserve (he's grown so civilized!), though all I wanted to was to know how his affairs ended so I can bear my pleasure in the certainty that it will pass.

I'm crying for the day when Zeus will not be holding me like this, or will be holding me like this while I am scheming how to inch myself out of the constriction of his arms. He doesn't ask me what's the matter. Think of all the women, mortal and the others, who've wept in Zeus's arms and he perhaps, when he was young, in theirs. He strokes my hair and keeps holding me. My tears grow cozy. For sophistication's sake I'll tell you the nature of ardor is to cool, but I can't believe it.

He's putting on his socks again, shaking each one methodically before he inserts his toes. I study him. From the minute he rises out of the sheets until he leaves by the front door at 7:20 he keeps his attention sideways to me: that way he can walk out of my room while I, still sensually attached, am drawn behind him. I stand in the doorway. He's profiled over the kitchen sink, letting the water run. Within the half hour, I had this man where a woman has her child, and now he's standing over there, by himself, he turns, opens the cupboard door—what's he looking for? He's choosing himself a glass, fills it, lifts it, tips it at the lip. I watch the water run into his mouth, see it hurdle the Adam's apple; now it's flowing down his inside, where I can't follow. Oh, fortunate Metis!

So that's how it is done! I can learn. I go and drink a glass of cold water too. It doesn't hurt. He's gone. On my way out I meet the super in the hallway and embrace him. "Sorry, my mistake!" I say, laughing. He hugs me and promises he'll fix my dripping faucet this very afternoon. "Thank you, you good man, you excellent super!" In the lobby I catch hold of the doorman's hand in both of mine. I press my cheek into his palm. We sit together on the front steps in the sunlight; he tells me about his boy doing nothing all day except sitting and watching TV, cutting his toenails. You can't tell with people, we say, you think this one's flipped out and next year you meet him and he's married, with a Plymouth. Three years later you hear that he's in Bellevue. These days you can never tell with young people.

I forgot to look at Zeus's hand again.

A letter. I get my magnifying glass to check this word, here, that looks like "love," and is. Don't look now: I think this is happiness. And Zeus, as I said, knows the weight of his words. When he writes "love" he knows what he means, what kind and how much, depending on the word that precedes and follows, the nearest mark of punctuation and its place in the body of the letter (sixth word of the second line in the second paragraph).

I run to the mirror, the way you might run to the corner to see the passing astronaut or what visiting royalty looks like, and it's me, and it seems reasonable to me that I'm Zeus's beloved.

I write him back stories, whole novels, juggling words for his entertainment, elated by my mastery, for these days

I can keep three, six, twelve perceptions and two mutually exclusive feelings in the air at one time, as well as a second-hand thought and a half, and a joke about juggling. "Oh, Love," I write him, and we both know I mean the kind unfreighted by workaday life. Never will he scrumple up his bathroom towel or I think to tell him not to put his shoes on the bedspread, for those are things that scuttle love when it is anchored in reality. Not Zeus and Lucinella! We make our arrangements. On the fifteenth I drive along the highways and freeways of America to motel row, Memphis, Tennessee. Humbert Humbert and Lolita slept here! Zeus has to leave at 7:20 the next morning, but in June there'll be a three-day conference in Jamaica.

I fly through the air to meet my love, leaving Kennedy at 6:15 a.m. The blue, red, and yellow lights, like chips of stained glass, spell the ground pattern that lifts us efficiently into the breaking dawn. We lean on the wing. The city slants radically up toward us and, with a long breath, settles back, spreading itself between the wide bodies of its waters, which ripple copper-colored, green, primrose. If we crash now, who would quarrel with so rich a death? The bellboy unlocks the door and he's already here, stretched on the bed . . .

Later that summer we go to Nîmes and take in a third-rate bullfight. We sleep over in Rome.

For my sake, Zeus agrees to a Swann's Tour of the Aegean. From our narrow bunk, we see through the port-hole the same, innumerable, nameless, little, rock-bound islands that Odysseus must have passed. In January we spend a Monday and Tuesday at the Sacher. We leave the tasseled curtains parted so we can see the old yellow stone of the back of the Vienna Opera from the baroque feather bed, and the next month in Barcelona, in Addis Ababa, Buenos Aires. There are beds everywhere. The world is our playground where we two accomplished lovers meet in mutual joy and without rancor sail our toy loves.

IX

If you can stand another party (this is the last one before the last one and there's to be a black magician at midnight and an exorcism at cockcrow):

Lucinella
requests the pleasure
of your company
to honor
Betterwheatling
on the publication
of
A Decade of Poetry, 1960–70
(Regrets only)

I'm always particularly fond of my friends when they're walking in my front door. It seems nice and a little ridiculous of them to leave their comfortable homes and come and stand around my living room. They hold their drinks. They turn their good, intelligent faces to one another and move their jaws up and down, Listen to the pleasant hiss and hum of innumerable conversations.

Happy and distraught, I move among my five novelists, four live poets (one of them eminent), six publishers, two agents, a writer of children's books, eleven critics, and a pair of gods.

"Hera! I didn't know you were in town!" I lie, while the back of my head charts the course Zeus is taking in the direction of the bar. "So! How have you been? How's Zeus?" I ask her.

"Waiting," she whispers, she leans toward me, "to become human. Ha! Ha!" We both laugh.

I'm astonished how expertly my vocal cords, jaws, gums, tongue, lips perform the motions of a woman chatting with an old friend at a party. I look around: who might be lying to *me?* Young Lucinella mumbles, "I am terrible! I haven't even read Betterwheatling's new book."

"You should," I tell her. (I'm studying the set of her jaw, the motion of her lips. Did she come with William? I didn't see him arrive.) "Betterwheatling is the best critic we have," I say. (Where does William sleep these nights? If it's in young Lucinella's bed, I would mind at the level where I shall mind my death.) "Come and meet him," I say.

"We've met," she says, "at Maurie's party and again at the symposium," but I interrupt what Betterwheatling is eagerly saying to Frank Friendling to say, "Betterwheatling, I want you to meet—I'm sorry, Lucinella, but I seem to have forgotten what your name is. This is my guest of honor . . . and now I've forgotten your name too, Betterwheatling."

"I'm Betterwheatling," says Betterwheatling. "Young Lucinella and I have met."

"And this is . . . ?"

"Friendling," says Friendling. "We all know each other, Lucinella."

"Then would you tell me what *my* name is, in case I have to introduce myself to someone."

"You are Lucinella," says Friendling.

"I'm afraid I haven't read your book," young Lucinella is telling Betterwheatling.

"It's a good book," I say, "and a beautiful piece of scholarship."

"Maurie thinks it's worthless," says Betterwheatling. "He wouldn't publish my afterword in *The Magazine*."

I see that Winterneet has brought his wife, the girl his mother picked for him, I'm sure, big, high-bosomed, high-shouldered, like one of the larger amphorae. He sits her down among the coats on my couch, and walks off.

I am the hostess and must go and talk to old Mrs. Winterneet. I can't tell if she is petrified by all those years with Winterneet, or stoned. Across her forehead file sixty-six gray hairs like the exemplary letter S the teacher draws on the top line of a second-grader's copy book, but I dare say she's a sterling and loyal wife, which is nothing to be snide about. There's much I could learn from Mrs. Winterneet if we could talk woman-to-woman, it's just that I have trouble remembering to keep listening to her telling me how Winterneet drives her to town every second and fifteenth of the month so she can see her doctor on East Eighty-ninth Street, in an even voice, just loud enough to drown out what Maurie is telling Winterneet. Seeing old Lucinella passing, I pull her sleeve. I say, "You know Mrs. Winterneet, of course!" and rise, obliging her to take my seat. She glares at me. Let the old ladies chat.

I join Maurie and Winterneet and say, "by the way, Maurie, why wouldn't you publish Betterwheatling's afterword in *The Magazine? I* think it's a beautiful book. The prose is so adroit—"

"I know," says Maurie. "That's why I published his foreword."

"Oh. Come and help me talk to Meyers," I say. Meyers is standing by the wall alone.

"I don't talk to Meyers!" says Maurie. "He no longer sends his poems to *The Magazine*."

I carry my drink across the room. Young Lucinella is telling Ulla she's sorry she's never read a word Ulla has written.

"Meyers!" I say. We sip our drinks. I don't have the stamina to wait till Meyers thinks of something to say, so I say, "You've hurt Maurie's feelings. Why don't you send your poems to *The Magazine?* "

"Because I haven't written any," Meyers says.

We sip our drinks. "Let's go and talk to Winterneet!" I say.

"The hell with Winterneet," says Meyers, showing his teeth behind his great, sad mustache. He raises his chin and cries, "Winterneet voted against my Pulitzer!"

I'm getting high and trot right over to Winterneet, who's putting his hand out to William, saying, "J. D. Winterneet. I don't believe we've met."

"We have *so!*" William cries, and stamps his foot. "At Maurie's on Thursday and again on Sunday, and at the Friendlings' party you told me you liked my poem, and in May we spent a weekend together at the symposium!"

"But if you remember, after that," says Winterneet, "at the Betterwheatlings' in September, I didn't know you again."

William raises his chin and from his exposed throat silently howls.

"Winterneet," I say, "how come you voted against Meyers's Pulitzer?"

"But that was fifteen years ago!" says Winterneet. "Since then he has become the most accomplished and interesting poet of the decade."

William says, "That's what Betterwheatling says in his new book."

"I have not read, nor do I intend to read, Betterwheatling's new book," says Winterneet.

"But Winterneet!" I say, "it's a beautiful piece of scholarship, the prose is adroit, and *I* think Betterwheatling is the best critic we have."

"I know he is!" wails Winterneet, "and he called me a dinosaur in the Sunday *Times*." ("I never even read the *Times*," young Lucinella mumbles at my back.) Winterneet unfolds a faded yellow clipping from his pocket, raises his chin, and reads: "J. D. Winterneet, that enormous walking fossil, the dinosaur of modern poetry."

My eyes glittering in my head, I go to find Betterwheatling.

"Betterwheatling, why did you call Winterneet a dinosaur in the Sunday *Times?*"

"You think he minded?" cries Betterwheatling. "I meant extinct but great. I think I said 'enormous.' *You* know I gave him a whole chapter in my new book."

And this is the moment when it hits me: I haven't *read* Betterwheatling's new book. Nor any of his other books either! As I stand in my amazement, staring into Betterwheatling's face, I can tell, with the shock of a certitude, by the set of the line of Betterwheatling's jaw, by the way his hair falls into his forehead, that Betterwheatling has never read a line I have written either and I flush with pain. I'll never invite *him* to another party!

The trouble with cutting up your friends is then you don't have them any more.

Betterwheatling

X

Midnight.

Enter Max Peters, the twelfth critic, whom I did not invite. Pavlovenka has brought him with her. She hugs me and whispers, "You don't mind! He had nowhere to go tonight."

"I never go to parties," Max says, out of the left corner of his mouth.

"I can't *stand* parties," I lie out of the right corner of mine and step in front of him to block from his vision what's going on right in my living room.

Max peers over my shoulder and spits.

I look over my shoulder too. And are these the friends I invited, six pages back, to come and talk with each other, and with me, because I liked them? What has changed my living room into this *New Yorker* cartoon full of chinless showoffs standing in groups or pairs? They turn their violent profiles on one another. Watch William's jaw move up and down, explaining publishing to fat Maurie, who picks his nose and nibbles his finger. His hand's shrunk to midget-size! Horrified, Winterneet looks into Ulla's wide-open mouth and Meyers backs into the wall before young Lucinella advancing to tell him the list of books ancient and modern, in English and foreign tongues, which she has not read.

Stout little Pavlovenka giggles, and squeals, "Don't you adore Max's outfit!" She points to his tall conical hat and makes nice-nice to the black stuff of his voluminous cloak. There's a rush of air past my cheek; Max has raised his arm and is pointing his bony forefinger between Betterwheatling's eyes. He says, "I just sent off my review of your new book, which I used as a peg for a discussion of this curious yearning to corral a lot of free-ranging poets into a ten-year period that begins and ends with zero. You, Betterwheatling, are quite the most distinguished of our Cowboy Critics."

Is Betterwheatling's solid flesh really dissolving or does it merely seem to fade like the Cheshire cat, which used to blow my mind until our fourth-grade visit to the science exhibition. "Press button to make lightwaves coincide, crest with crest and trough with trough, so that they cancel themselves out," read Miss Norris, our science teacher, from the card glued to the wall of the display case inside which a red rubber hot-water bottle was slowly, slowly disappearing. "How come?" we asked. "How come Ulla always gets to press the button?" "Don't lean on the glass," Miss Norris said. "Is it going to come back?" we asked her.

It is the power of the epigram, if it's true, or mean enough, or bawdy, or rhymes or alliterates, to become a permanent attribute, and henceforward, if Betterwheatling comes back and we find ourselves face-to-face at parties, I will see him—through a secret smile—on horseback, lassoing maverick poets.

So much for Betterwheatling, whom I had rather a tendency to be in love with.

I move a little closer to Max Peters, to be on the safe side, and duck to avoid his rising arm. It's William walking toward us with his hand out to shake Max's forefinger.

"So, Max!" William says. "How's excellence? How's mediocrity these days?"

"Cruelly far apart as ever," Max Peters says. "And you, William, have you discovered your place in the gap? Or are you still hoping to turn out to be Shakespeare?"

"Who says I'm not!" cries William. (Already his face pales.) "As a poet my powers are in their infancy."

"And what you can't bear is to grow up and be William."

On the spot where my poor husband stood in his dear and aggravating flesh, tan shoes, slacks, polo shirt, stands another epigram. And it's apt! Max, I never said that you were stupid, but what can William do with this piece of truth except add it to the arsenal of personal disasters he stores in his Underground, with which to prick himself on to despair on his off days; when he's been successful in bed at night and written well all morning, he won't believe, won't remember what it was you said.

(You understand, of course, I say none of this out loud to Max. I've crept in under the destroyer's shadow.)

Max is pointing where Bert's footballer's shoulders hulk flirtatiously over the furiously pretty girl.

"Poet from New Jersey!" Max spits.

Bert's gone.

Max points at Zeus and Hera. "A couple of anachronisms!" he says, and they disappear. My party is thinning!

Frightened, I clutch Max's cloak. "There's Winterneet!" I whisper.

"Where?" I point. Max says, "I thought he died back in 1896. There's old Lucinella. She died in 1968. And young

Lucinella, who's a dog." I part the front edges of Max's cloak and slip inside. Out of the darkness I prompt: "How about Ulla?"

"What about me?" asks Ulla.

"You're a tart," Max says.

"So old-fashioned!" says Ulla. It's true. Max is a moral man.

He says, "You're our West Side Alma Mahler. You once had the nation's most valuable collection of near-geniuses under your belt."

"*Had!*" cries Ulla and begins to fade.

"While your career," he says, and points at Maurie, "depends on standing on your writers' shoulders, alternatively with your foot on one or another of their necks."

Ulla and Maurie have disappeared.

"Let *me* try one!" I say, and part the edges of Max's cloak like the flaps of a tent. Disentangling my forefinger from the complication of the folds, I point at Meyers. It's not at all a matter of dislike, or of any harm done me that I might be wishing to avenge; on the contrary, I've always had, and have at this moment, the warmest feeling toward him. I want to make it positively clear: this avidity which flushes my cheek, accelerates my pulse, and draws my breath in great, bowing strokes across my heart is motivated by no self-serving, no purpose whatsoever. It is the purest form of malice for malice's sake with which I point my forefinger at Meyer's trembling mustache and say, "You zombie, you!"

I saw Meyers's rabbit eyes register surprise and terror before he disappeared.

But I'm unsatisfied. I botched that. What talentless abuse! It would take me weeks of revision to frame some triumphant nastiness. I am only an apprentice. Like everything else, it needs practice, practice, practice. "Pavlovenka, you middle-aged giggle!" I call out. Better, but still needs shaping, sharpening.

It's not nice to stare, I know, but how fascinating to watch Pavlovenka's lips struggling for some suitable expression. Anger never occurs to her, and once a mouth becomes conscious of itself, it is no longer capable of expressing nothing. Pavlovenka keeps uncertainly giggling. Meanwhile, the slopes, promontories, depressions by which we recognize that this is Pavlovenka's face lose confidence in their definitions and relationships. Look how the eyes overgrow their boundaries, becoming two great black abysms that open into Pavlovenka's Underground, which we have no business seeing. Max, that's what I meant about telling truths in public. An instant has stripped away the character it took forty years to piece together. Why do you think she took up poetry? Yes, I've read it, Max, I know, she likes everything pretty. But, Max, there's gallantry in refusing to let her disability handicap a naturally cheerful and affectionate disposition, blessed with a lot of useful energy. As a teacher of poetry workshops, she does her homework better than some I might mention, is generous to her students with time and attention; a tireless judge, according to her own best lights, of scholarships, grants, and prizes; a frequent and cheerful panelist on symposia; a loquacious radio and public-television interviewee; and an active member of PEN who writes letters to foreign powers urging the release of imprisoned intellectuals; and by keeping herself busy from the moment she becomes conscious in the morning and puts on those terrible striped stockings to distract the eye, and winds her braids tightly round her ears, she has (except for a nervous breakdown in her late thirties) kept herself from acknowledging, and believed that she had kept the world from suspecting, what I had to go and say out loud just now, in front of her oldest friends, who've known from the first five minutes they spent in her company that Pavlovenka is a fool and a bore.

There, in Pavlovenka's stead, stands a stout little giggle,

poor Cheshire pussy, poor Pavlovenka, whom I have known since that first time at Yaddo—how many years ago! I'll miss her.

Why does Max look at *me!* Angels and ministers of grace! There is no one else left, except a crowd of aphorisms, shifting and rustling at my back.

Quickly I assume the expressive posture of female sculpture in periods when art is on the decline. Imagine me naked from the waist up (below is draped in a sheet). My stone feet are planted, knees loose, back arching away from Max's slowly rising arm. I spread my fingers before my eyes to shield them against the imminence of a terrible enlightenment, and quickly, before Max opens his mouth, I begin to rattle off my sins, from the deepest treachery down to my least stupidity, dishonesty of mind, shabbiness of feeling (footnoting each with mitigating circumstances as well as evidence to the contrary), including evils I am not particularly prone to and have never committed but probably will (nothing human being alien to me). I mark off each item according to Jewish tradition with a thump of the fist on the breast. My exhausted conscience pauses for breath, and in that moment Max has pronounced my sentence. I hope it's a good one—terse, witty, balanced. If one's to be an epigram, it would be nice to have stylistic distinction. Because of the roar of my listening I never heard what it was he said. Now I know what a Cheshire cat feels like. The parts with least bulk are first to go. Already I can look right through my pinkie, though the palm is barely translucent. Knuckles and the thumb stay densest longest. Oh, Max! This isn't anybody, this is different, this is ME disappearing—my childhood, Ulla at school, all those application forms to colleges, and going, and having gone, and Maurie publishing my poem; and the poem I was always going to write in my new notebook, fucking William and oh! Zeus!

And reading *Emma* over and over! Melanctha! Lear. Bach. There go my toes. HELP ME!

The cock crows—or was that the doorbell ringing?

A beneficent breeze wafts through the smoke-filled room and animates the poor walking epigrams. They quiver like so many compass needles toward the two who have newly entered.

George and Mary Friend don't stand out at a party at first. Maybe their clothes are a little grayer, the color of their faces fresher, coming from out of town.

"Quick, Max, a boon," I whisper. "Don't tell George and Mary—what it was you said about me."

Max laughs. "They know."

"No, they don't!" I cry. "They can't, or in all the years we have been friends I would have intercepted a glance. There has never been a hint—"

"But, my dear Lucinella! Why would it occur to them to mention to you or out loud to each other what's as plain as the nose in the middle of your face?"

"Dear god! Max! Are you telling me that everybody knows my nose!"

George and Mary, stopping to greet old friends, seem not to notice the predicament in which they find them. I would run to meet them but my feet are gone, my knees going. "Mary!" I cry. "Here I am! George!"

"Max Peters's been on the rampage, I see," says Mary. She takes my hand and chafes my absent fingers. "Shall I go spit in his eye for you?"

"Shush, dear," says George.

"Look what he did to my party!"

"They'll be all right," says George. "As soon as they hit the cold air outside, they'll start to reconstitute. By tomorrow morning they'll be themselves again."

"Tomorrow morning!" Mary says. "It took you a good

month to recover from Winterneet's review of your last book. Poor Winterneet!" she says. "He looks terrible."

George says, "It gets harder as you get older."

"Let's go over and cheer him up," I suggest.

"I'm not talking to Winterneet," says George. "He thought my last book was worthless."

"It wasn't only Max," I say. "Betterwheatling called Winterneet a dinosaur, and it was I who called Meyers a zombie and Pavlovenka a middle-aged giggle. I don't know why I did, I'm not really vicious! I mean we're all of us perfectly decent people."

"Your error," says George, "is in the colloquial use of 'really' and 'perfectly' in quasi-logical proposition."

"George, don't be pompous," Mary says.

"No, go on!" I say. "That's interesting!"

"Your viciousness to Meyers and Pavlovenka," George says, "proves you to be 'really,' though by no means 'perfectly,' or even preponderantly, vicious. You are preponderantly, but by no means perfectly, decent."

"Oh brother!" Mary says.

"He's right. That's true!" I say, conscious of a shy happiness in George and Mary's protracted attention. Afraid I might begin to bore them, I make a quarter turn to give them a chance to decamp. I lower my eyes and see their feet planted: they're not going anywhere; their toes point toward mine, which are beginning to return through every stage of transparence, via translucence, to their old solidity. The wholesome influence of a calm and sober friendship renatures me. I'm turning back into a person. I look over my shoulder to see who is behind me whom George and Mary would not rather be talking with and see Max Peters advancing and holler, "No, you don't! These two you're not going to get. Quick, George! Duck, Mary!" But Mary points a forefinger at the forefinger Max points at her, and says,

"When you get nasty, Max, a tiny blob of spittle tends to form at the right corner of your mouth."

Max's arm sinks, his chin rises. From his exposed throat is torn Don Giovanni's last, great chromatic howl sliding an octave down from high D. He covers his eyes with his black sleeve, lifts a knee, and, like Rumpelstiltskin hearing himself named, crashes through the floor and is never seen again.

One by one my unfortunate guests find their coats on my couch and leave.

"I'm sorry," I say to them. I cry a little.

"Don't," says Betterwheatling kindly, kissing me goodbye. "We're pros, Lucinella. We know a survival trick or two."

"Like what?" I ask him.

"I can always argue that my critic is a knave or a fool, incapable of understanding the nature of my work, or jealous, or angry with me for some real or imagined affront to himself or a friend. Since I frequently agree with Peters's judgments, I shall take the impregnable position that the world is behind, ahead, or out of the mainstream of my thinking, else how could it continue on its appointed round, at its usual speed, when this is My Publication Day? And now I'm going home to bed, Lucinella, because tomorrow morning I start on my new book, *Poetry of the Seventies*. It fortunately really is the work that matters. Thank you for a lovely party."

"Goodbye," George says.

"Don't everybody leave me!" I cry, and he and Mary sit down on my couch. We talk. Once in a while George says, "I've got to write in the morning." But still we talk.

George has fallen asleep on my couch. Mary and I talk till the sun comes up. Then they go home.

I'm too tired to sleep. And I'm out of coffee.

A page of *The New York Times* wheels up to Broadway before me, slowly, with a lovely motion.

The new white light catches a pool of dog piss. The brilliance breaks the heart.

"So what's to smile about?" asks the grocer.

"Nothing. Some friends were over," I say, "and we talked."

The grocer gives me an apple for a present, he says, because I look happy.

Zeus arrives today. It is our anniversary. He asks, "What shall I give you, Lucinella?"

Dumbfounded, I wonder: What does one ask of a retired god?

"Shall I show myself to you," he offers, "in my glory?"

"Great heavens, no!" I cry, remember what happened to Semele. (Once I peeked, and saw his face in mid-passion hanging above me, and quickly closed my eyes.)

"Would you like me to translate you among the stars?" he asks, and I'm tempted. The constellation of Lucinella the Poet, in the heavens for all eternity. "That's not what I want!" I say, surprised. I'd rather thought it was.

"Ask me for something," he says. He rises, comes toward me, embraces me, though it's already 7:15. Still I hesitate.

"What, what?" he asks. I am afraid. "What, love?" He kisses me.

"Become human for me," I whisper rapidly, so he won't hear what I am saying. He throws his head back and laughs and kisses me delightedly as if I'd said something superlatively witty. We're both laughing. Still he holds me. This is our anniversary.

It is 7:20.

THE END

Ulla calls on the telephone. "There's going to be a block party in Times Square on the twenty-second. Big blast! Hope it doesn't rain! Are you coming?" she asks me.

"Not with you, I'm not," I say.

"Why?" cries Ulla. "What did I do?"

"You put me in your novel," I say.

"Did I say something unkind or untrue?" she says. "You come off perfectly interesting and nice!"

"I know," I say, and hang up on her. How could Ulla make me into a minor character with walk-on in Chapter VIII and one eleven-line speech at the very end, when it's obvious the protagonist is me.

And so she washed the soot off her face and hands, opened the walnut . . .

XI

The block party is on the twenty-second. That gives me ten days to shape up.

First, my fingernails. How can the millennium come as long as my hands are dirty? There are people I know whose fingers always have that washed look. They think, "Lucinella has dirty fingernails," because they don't understand my life's object, along with learning French, is to get my fingers as pink as new soap. So this morning I have a bath without reading and soak my hands in the hot water before going down to the Whole Earth Shop at the corner, where a young man with sweet, smudgy eyes, in a Mickey Mouse shirt and hair tied in a ribbon, like Mozart, sells the American flag at half-mast, hand-woven blue-jeans made into mini muumuus, and jars of organic brewer's yeast. I buy one.

Next morning, after I soak my fingernails, I eat a healthy heaping tablespoonful of brewer's yeast before I take the bus downtown to Siegfried's Salon on Madison, very chic—all slate and mirrors. I'm assigned to Mr. Andre. He runs his fingers through my hair and gags. He asks me if

I regularly exercise my hair. "Look at mine," he says. "For fifteen minutes every morning, I bend each separate strand forward three times, back three times, side three." Mr. Andre snips. I was wrong to think it was my hair that made him gag. It's me. But I refuse to reciprocate. I can appreciate that fourteen-inch waist, the yellow pants, those twin grapefruits operating inches from my cheeks, in their own terms.

"Ginny!" Mr. Andre kisses a beautiful blonde.

"Have!" Ginny says. She feeds Mr. Andre bites of glazed doughnut.

Mr. Andre twirls her around and says, "I like, I like!"

Ginny's golden hair is sculptured in three chevrons across a forehead which is rosy brown, as if lit from within, though I am sure she has no soul. How does she come by that pure line of jaw? I know where my heart grows because I feel it cramp with envy and pleasure.

"So? How was the audition?" Mr. Andre asks.

"Oh god!" cries Ginny. "What if I *get* it! I think I'm *pregnant!*"

"*God!*" cries Mr. Andre. "*No!* Listen," he says, "I'll see you in Times Square on the twenty-second. Stunning girl." He's talking to me! I'm pleased. "Very talented. She's auditioning for a Pepsi commercial."

"There's a poem of mine in this magazine, on page 36," I tell Mr. Andre. He doesn't say he'll see me in Times Square. He twirls my chair, hands me a mirror, and, like a circus artist after his bravura stunt, poses with his back arched, hand extended to my head. I applaud. "Fabulous!" I say. But under my right eye I see the sign that copy editors use to indicate a new paragraph, which this morning I took to be the imprint of my pillow.

So next morning, after I soak my nails, and eat a wholesome tablespoonful of brewer's yeast, and exercise my hair for fifteen minutes, I take the bus to Princess Romanoff, upstairs, on Fifth Avenue, for a free skin analysis.

The décor is wall-to-wall pink Leatherette trimmed with gilt Louis Quatorze. A large, mature girl levels her eyes at the point just below where they would meet mine. Though she too was born, suffers daily to come by that flat stomach at her age, and, like me, will die, we travel by such different routes she doesn't like me. I can always tell.

By the authority vested in her white coat, she turns a purple light onto my face, which turns green. She enters a number on a chart. She flays a square inch of skin off my forehead and spins it in a tiny centrifuge. It disintegrates. She enters a second number, collates both with a slide rule, and determines that I need a treatment.

"Which won't make the slightest difference, as you and I know!" I say, smiling into her eyes. I don't want to have her think I'm taken in.

She does not smile back. She says, "In seven days you'll be a different woman."

Just in time for the twenty-second.

I invite her to the block party.

In a clinical white cell an old, motherly Roumanian tucks me under an eiderdown and douses every light except where her face leans upside down over mine.

Multiple fingers descend my cheek to my chin.

"What's that for?" I ask her.

"Is for relax," she says. "Is pleasant?"

"Very . . . " I say.

Steam rises.

"Smells like my grandmother's kitchen," I say.

"Is prune tea," she says, " like enema your skin, relax very heavy now, for clean out your pores."

What's this sharp coolness that prickles on my cheek, I ask her.

"Is lemon I put for ascorbic and vitamin C. Close your eyes very relax."

"That feels like butter on my forehead," I say drowsily.

"*Is* butter. For alkali butter soft your skin and smooth vitamin A."

"And the sticky stuff?"

"Honey, to make sweet and golden, mix with yolk of egg like baby chicken, a younger, fluffier you. Go yourself very heavy now, very relax, nourish masque for thirty minutes."

Relaxed, almost asleep, I hear two voices whispering and open my eyes. The yellow, old, shriveled peasant face floats upside down into my line of vision and says, "Pleasant all right?"

"Very pleasant," I say and close my eyes.

Softly, softly, the two foreign whispers laugh in my darkness.

Next morning, when I have soaked my fingernails, eaten my brewer's yeast, and exercised my hair for fifteen minutes, I apply a concentrate of prune, lemon, butter, honey, and egg, with the admixture of a splinter of the True Cross at $34.98 an ounce, and leave it on my face for half an hour, so that I barely make it to Dr. Treublau on time.

The doctor's office has the dowdy richness of Persian carpet, leather books, and old, large, bad oils in their massive golden frames. "What would you like to talk about today?" he asks me.

"Why I am feeling happy."

"Anything else?"

"Why I keep liking everyone I meet."

"Whom do you like?"

"Everybody. All the poets at Yaddo, a gay hairdresser, voluptuous young girls both black and white, and my phony Roumanian beautician, and you too, Dr. Treublau," I say, because he seems very beautiful. His El Greco hands are folded in an attitude of prayer, pointing downward on his stomach, his chin on his dry old chest, face elongated with listening.

"And why do you think you like all these people?"

"Because," I say—am I going to cry?—"I don't want them blown up."

"Will they be blown up?" he asks.

"Are you kidding, Doctor?" I point around at his furnishings from Vienna of the thirties translated to East Seventy-second Street. "Our mothers started to get us ready as infants. We had biennial dental and ophthalmological checkups, were taught our manners and virtues, went through a liberal education, traveled, read, had friends, made love, and now there's only four days left to get my nails clean, stomach flat, hair styled, skin and psyche in condition for the big blast in Times Square."

I recognize the shadow passing across the doctor's eye—or is it a temporary lightening of the absorption with which he listens? Dr. Treublau is waiting for me to stop showing off.

"Have you a dream that you want to tell me?"

"Yes," I say. "Though it's a cheap fictional device for sneaking in one's point."

A shadow crosses the doctor's eye.

"In this dream I'm sitting in something . . . in a boat . . . like a gondola, with some people . . . "

"Who are the people?"

"I haven't the foggiest notion . . . except they're people I love, my ex-husband, William, and young Lucinella, his mistress, who'll be okay when she gets over her protracted adolescence. Doctor, what happened to the brassy chippies who used to shanghai our husbands? And there's my ex-lover, Zeus, and his wife, who's even smarter and nicer than he is. Where are the bores and harridan wives whose husbands we used to liberate?"

Dr. Treublau is waiting. "What happens in your dream?"

"We're facing downstream, toward the city. I'm crying. I plead with my mother or whoever it is in a white coat standing just out of sight behind my left shoulder. I can't understand why she will not stop them from blowing the beautiful city up."

"And what do you think this blow-up means?" the doctor asks.

"The Big Bomb," I say.

"What else?"

"Doomsday? The Second Coming? The Meshiach!"

"And what else?" he asks. "This explosion you're asking your mother or some figure in a doctor's white coat of authority to stop?"

"The Great Orgasm! Of course!" I cry excitedly, because now I see how this chapter is going to end. I blush.

"That explanation bothers you?"

"Oh, for heaven's sake," I cry. What modern woman would be caught dead blushing at sex. "I'm embarrassed by the way my symbols dovetail, and annoyed, because you won't believe that is the cause."

"That's all for today," he says. He wants me to dream him a dream every day.

So next morning, when I've soaked my nails, taken my yeast, exercised my hair, and masqued my face, I go back to bed and dream a dream, and have to run all the way to my French lesson, with only three days to go, so next morning I study my verbs in my bath and after bending my hair this way and that a bit, I can't do my skin because I got tired of brewer's yeast and ate my masque for breakfast and can't dream a thing with this nervous sense I have of time running out, and next morning I'm so demoralized I don't feel like bathing at all, the hell with my hair, I've been a slob all my life and now it is too late, I'll never learn French now!

William calls. Would I meet him in Times Square tomorrow. I am the one he loves, he says, and has all along.

XII

For weeks the city has been sprucing up the area in preparation for the block party on the twenty-second.

The Allstate Insurance eagle flaps its neon wings on high, and Mickey Mouse, so cleverly constructed out of bulbs of light, runs, stops, does a double-take, and continues running. The Marlboro man—a good father and provider, one can tell—blows his eternal smoke rings through the perfect cardboard circle of his mouth.

Tonight traffic has been diverted and Times Square handed over to its citizens for a public celebration.

Garlands of pennants connect the street lamps. Their posts are vomit-colored with bands of yellowish-lilac, blackish, greenish, and orange paint, contributed by the private sector through a collection instituted by the Police Athletic League as a project for the metropolitan schoolchildren, who got time off from lessons. If the brushwork is messy, it's the "Neighborhood Spirit," which is the theme of this day.

The invitation moves on a crawl around the three sides of the old Times building: . . . EVERYBODY WELCOME TO THE BIG BLAST ON TIMES SQUARE . . . FIND YOUR FRIENDS . . . MEET

PEOPLE YOU HAVE NEVER MET BEFORE . . . THREE ROCK BANDS . . . BOOTHS . . . BARGAINS . . . A MOBILE ROLLER COASTER FOR THE KIDS . . . ETHNIC GOODIES FROM AROUND THE WORLD . . . RAFFLES . . . PRIZES . . . AND A GRAND MIDNIGHT SURPRISE . . .

The first rock band, which calls itself the Spheres, plugs itself into the electricity. My eardrums burst and inhibition suppurates. I spread my arms to the family of Puerto Ricans drinking beer in a window on the second floor. "Come down!" I call to them. "Come and join us!" cry all the people in the street around me. The young man in BVD's turns to the woman leaning her arms on the windowsill. She laughs. At us? Or didn't they understand? We make great pantomime motions with our arms, meaning "Come!" Are they too shy? Now the street door opens and a little boy bursts out and scuttles across the street, where the children stand around the wonderfully blaring Spheres.

The kids, supplied with fat sticks of colored chalk, draw clowns and elephants and write FUCK YOU in letters reaching from sidewalk to sidewalk.

Where in all this crush will I find William?

There's the Contact paper man with his wife and children. My super! My doorman! "Hi!" I say to them all. Here's the old floor scraper. I tell him, "You were quite right about the sealer," and nod my head up and down. "How are you?" I say to the Fuller brush man who sold me the millennium, and to the grocer who gave me an apple, when I was happy. "Mr. Andre!" I say shyly. "Hello!" he cries in the friendliest fashion. We kiss. He twirls me. "You see," he says, "what exercise did for your follicles!" It's true! And before I left home I looked in the mirror and saw the sign of the new paragraph under my right eye definitely fuzzier, I think.

From the sidewalk an elegant hand waves. Dr. Treblau, you! All the way from Vienna to come to a block party in Times Square! He steps forward and, just like a regular person, kisses me on the cheek.

Here's Maurie's Book Booth. "How's the poetry moving?"

"They won't even steal it," Maurie says sadly.

"Winterneet! What are *you* selling?"

"Live poets reading from their work," says Winterneet. "Handshakes are ten cents extra," he says to a woman with a manuscript under her arm. She says, "I've come all the way from Nebraska. Do you do it on a typewriter, with a ball-point pen or pencil? Mornings or at night? Facing any particular direction?"

Winterneet says, "Interviews $2.50 for five minutes. Did you know," he says, turning to me, "that William won the Times Square Prize for the Best Younger Poet? It's to be presented at the midnight ceremonies."

"William? The Best Younger Poet!" I cry, delighted but surprised. "He himself told me his poetry was worthless. Winterneet, you're sure it was William who got the prize?"

"I'm one of the judges," says Winterneet.

"But, Winterneet, whenever you meet William at a party you don't remember who he is, and Maurie ignores him."

"Maurie was the other judge," says Winterneet.

"Where *is* William? I want to congratulate him. Newman! Good to see you. You didn't come to my party."

"Hello, Lucinella," says Newman and steps on my right toe. "I'm sorry!" I say. He steps on my left toe.

"Where are you going?" I ask, walking beside him.

"To the Black Booth under the sign of the Raised Fist."

"Hi!" I say to our stage manager. The lovely black Wedgwood girl with the two-by-two-foot topiary Afro is passing out cookies to the little children; those eleven and over are lined up on the left for their hand grenades with mini hydrogen warheads.

"Have you seen William?" I inquire at the Women's Booth.

"The hell with William," says Cilena Betterwheatling.

Ulla holds out her hands to me, but I put mine behind my back. "I'm not talking to you," I say, surprised.

Ulla looks unhappy. She says, "I thought you were kidding!"

"So did I!" I say.

"Come and join us," say Pavlovenka and Alice Friendling and the furiously pretty girl.

"I will," I say. "But first I've got to go find William and congratulate him on winning the prize for the Best Younger Poet."

"Which you'd have got, if you were a man!" Cilena cries.

"Fuck the whole lot of them. None of them, is what I mean," shrieks Alice.

It's not that I'm not tempted by the feminist mystique. Oh, for the blessings of anger! To have the trouble identified, once and for all, to know whose fault it is! Except that commits one to battle. "Forgive me," I tell them. "It's not that I don't love you all, it's just that I tend to resist conversions."

Already the sky is darkening. The street lights have come on.

What is it that keeps butting me in the shins? I look down. There's a swarthy, bearded man without arms or legs, strapped on a rolling platform three inches off the ground. Why here, where the crowd is thickest? If he gets trampled, it will be *his* fault, I think, annoyed. "Watch where you're going," he snarls. His strong yellow teeth control the kind of switch that operates electric trains. He stops, backs up, reverses, and rams me, again and again. He's clearing a path for a man and woman who converse deftly with fingers, palms, wrists, their faces tense with animation, mouths wide in voiceless hilarity. The woman lofts her sign, which says

We don't care
if you stare
O.L.

She glares. Why at me? I'm very sympathetic.

Behind them comes a skinny girl in a little white skirt. The gold braid on her peaked hat spells

The amputee
you see
has a chance
to dance
O.L.

Balanced on one leg, she twirls her crutch in the air, catches it, and stumps on. Behind her a pair of Mongoloids waltz around and around.

The twisted boy who follows wears a sweat shirt on which it says

The cripples
all
are having
a ball
O.L.

He ducks his head with a back-down-sideways motion, never quite in step, nor exactly alternating with the crossing of one foot over the other, in a syncopation that is out of time with any rhythm this world can make out, and marches, eyes fixed in terror, into the press of people coming toward him.

The geriatric case who brings up the rear turns her eager pinhead, like a bespectacled, super-intelligent chicken, this way and that. There's something about the excellent cut of her sparse hair, a familiarity about the subtle browns of the dress . . .

She sees me and waves her sign on which is written

A poet who searched throughout Asia
For the word that she'd lost in aphasia
Found it here all the time,
Where it scans with her rhyme—
And her reason? To please and amaze ya.

O.L.

"It's old Lucinella, isn't it?" I ask her.

She nods. "Official CCRG poet."

"What's CCRG?"

"Cripples' Conch-shell Raisin . . . " she says and shakes her head. Her arms make the charade player's repeated urgent motion to draw my comprehension toward herself. "Conch-shell Raisin Group."

"Cripples' Consciousness Raising Group?" I suggest.

Right right right, she nods, her eyes happy with the triumph of communication.

"You probably should catch up with your friends," I say, "but I've always wondered: does the malfunction of language tell you anything about the way it works?"

She nods eagerly, yes yes, holds up a forefinger for my attention, points to her head, and bends the forefinger to make a ring with the thumb.

"The head is round? Is a ring?'

No no no. Come on, come on, she motions with her arms.

"A circle? Zen!"

Come on, come on.

"Is okay? The head . . . the *thinking* is okay!"

Right right right. Attend: she points to her throat and repeats the sign of the ring.

"And speaking is okay."

Right right. Attend: she moves her fore- and middle fingers with a scissor action across her face.

"But they don't connect. What a brutal affliction for a poet!"

Brutal, right, right, she nods. "But so *inter*stiting . . . interstriating . . . interspersing . . . " She shakes her head, laughs, and, urgently holding up one finger of her right hand, taps four left fingers on the wrist.

"One word. Four syllables," I say. "First two syllables, 'inter.' Third syllable . . . "

Old Lucinella closes her eyes and puts her cheek on her horizontal palm.

"I'm afraid you may miss your friends," I say worriedly.

Come on come on come on.

"Sleep? Rest! Interest! Interesting!"

Right right right right. "It is all so . . . " Old Lucinella stretches and turns her scaly, ancient neck like a turtle this way and that. She lifts her arms, points all around at the sky that has turned as black as black, at the Times building crawl, which says: . . . 11:55 . . . PROBABILITY OF SHOWER ACTIVITY . . . 11:56 . . . at the life-insurance eagle flapping neon red, Mickey Mouse, all the prettily lighted booths, and at the crowd, the inexplicable current of its movements: *New York!* Behind the owl spectacles on the great emaciated beak of her nose, old Lucinella's eyes are suffused. "It's so immensely, it's all so intersticing . . . " She shakes her head.

"I really think maybe you'd better go."

Right right. She waves to me and trots after the other cripples.

"Benjamin, for heaven's sake! I haven't seen you since the party at Maurie's."

"So, Lucinella," Ben says, "this is the right party at last?"

"At last, Benjamin. This is the big blast!" I say. "And only one minute more till midnight."

I see George and Mary in the crowd. I ask them, "How do you handle being frightened?"

George says, "By thinking of Last Things." Mary says, "Making applesauce." But it's too late for that now. There goes the twelve o'clock siren, and I hear the screaming. At the edge of the crowd, people begin to run. I feel my flesh curdle—it must be from the radiation already released into the air, so now I don't have to worry any longer what it is that's going to happen. Now it has happened, I can breathe blissfully, and I raise my head and see Meyers. I ask him, "Why do I feel so euphoric?" Meyers says, "Euphoria is the flip side of disaster." He's looking up too. "It's a direct hit," he says.

At the top of the Times building boils a mass of blackish-brown bubbles that crowd each other out and shoot upwards with such a roaring that the little Puerto Rican boy with his shirt blasted off him, his arms hanging, his mouth as wide as it will open, seems to be crying on a silent screen. He rocks on the balls of his feet, wailing, wailing.

Where's his mother? I look up to the second-floor window and see the wall crack, lean, and crumble toward me. The sky's on fire.

"Now I understand!" I say to Betterwheatling, who's appeared beside me. "Of course! The Rose, the Fire, the Bomb, and the Great Orgasm, they're all one."

Betterwheatling smiles and looks not through his glasses but down his nose at me, and he says, "You're such a romantic."

"A romantic! Me?" I cry. I'm upset.

Betterwheatling points his umbrella at the blackish-brown cloud as it is about to mushroom. It turns out to be the retractable kind, stops billowing, and reverses like a genie tricked back into its bottle. The young Puerto Rican father has come out of the street door in his BVD's, tucks his little yelling, kicking boy under his arm, and carries him into the house.

I look to the edge of the crowd where the screaming people are still running. They are holding newspapers over their heads and duck squealing and laughing into the subway entrance to get out of the sudden rain. Betterwheatling has unfolded his umbrella over both of us, and I start being frightened again.

"Here you are!" William says. "Are you hungry? Let's go get something at the Melting Pot Booth."

"By the way," I say, "William, do *you* think I'm a romantic? It isn't even my idea. I mean, it's all Dr. Treublau and T.S. Eliot. William, I almost forgot! Did you really get the Times Square Prize for the Best Younger Poet?'

"I did indeed," William says. "Lucinella, do you think I *am?*"

"Absolutely!" I answer him. "Pass me a marinated mushroom, please."

I scramble up his trouser leg into his jacket pocket and poke out my head. "I've just learned how to handle terror," I say.

"How?" William asks.

"By remembering I have to die," I say, and close the flap over my head.

XIII

"Lucinella dead? Impossible! There must be some mistake. I saw her in Times Square only yesterday and she was alive, I know, because I stood as close to her as I am to you now, and we were talking."

"Well, she is dead; died in the early hours of the morning in William's pocket through absolutely no fault of his. She climbed in herself. The funeral is at eleven."

"Well, well. If the funeral is at eleven, then Lucinella must be dead."

Please, William, put me in a plain pine box, not one of those polished jobs, and use the difference to buy yourself a comfortable chair to sit in or take a trip to Greece for me, William, it's pleasure that will keep you grieving, I'll be so absent. Besides, I like plain pine, if it isn't waxed or varnished, though I guess they'd better apply a coat of sealer. I like the *idea* of a final community with worms but not the practice. Or can I learn, like the Ancient Mariner, and bless maggots?

Keep the casket closed; no open casket, my nose is too long. And let there be Bach. They may mention god so long as it's in Hebrew. See if you can stop the rabbi speaking English unless he is a poet, which isn't probable.

Now that I'm wearing my plain pine, it docs feel skimpy; one part of me always craved splendor.

It's not a bad turnout. William, his chin pale and mottled, looks like a man after a heavy illness, and J. D. Winterneet's eyes are red. Thank you, Winterneet, for minding. Now his whole face flushes with the effort to keep himself from smiling. It's all right, Winterneet, don't worry if my death excites you. Feel what you feel what you feel. I used to worry that I never wept appropriately at death but cried at anything by Bach; synagogues and churches indiscriminately made me swallow tears, I think, as if there'd been a promise broken. Maybe Bach is the promise kept?

The music stops and we are on our own again.

"*Adonai nasan, Adoinai lakach.* The Lord giveth and the Lord taketh away," says the rabbi. "We are gathered together this morning to mourn the passing of Lucinella, poet, author, woman, a young woman much loved, to judge from the number of you gathered here today."

(Strike the second "gathered." Keep those Bible rhythms out of your modern prose and use your *ear*, Rabbi! If you say "this morning" you can't say "to mourn.")

"Poetry is a hard taskmaster," the rabbi says.

(Much he knows. How many minutes is he supposed to go on talking?)

"It is the poet's sacred task to keep his eye on his own heart and on the pulse of the nation, for it is he who, if I may be allowed to coin a phrase, must hold the mirror up to nature. But there comes to all of us the night when we must call it a day. The farmer hangs up his scythe, the scientist washes his test tube, the banker locks his vault, and

Lucinella covers her typewriter for the last time, and God the Great Critic says, 'Daughter, how have you used the talent I have given you?' Lucinella answers him and says, 'Success did not ruin me, neither did failure make me falter. The critic's cruel pen did not turn me from my path nor did his praise unduly raise me up.' And the Father says, 'Well done, Daughter,' stand and say after me, '*Yisgadal veyiskadash . . .* ' "

Bach is back. God, let me not be dead.

The last mourner has filed out. They switch off the phonograph, put me in the elevator, take me down and out the back door into the waiting hearse. (I always rather admired efficiency.) The driver hops in. We're going east. There are a lot of nursing homes on Seventy-third Street. The wheelchairs are out this May morning. We turn north along the park and stop, I imagine, to let people pile into the limousines.

Betterwheatling, once, walking me around the lake at Yaddo, said my thoughts were natury. That's funny, Betterwheatling, but look at those chartreuse leaves—buds of leaf! In one week the park will be thick and green. I remember reading about a letter left by a suicide who said in spring she longed to push the flowers back into the ground.

We're moving. Seventy-seventh Street, where Maurie and Ulla live, right across from the museum. The names of the famous dead are engraved in Roman capitals around the façade: Pasteur, Pythagoras, Darwin, Einstein . . . lest we forget. Why do those animals in glass cases, stuffed by experts to look as if caught in mid-motion, look so dead?

That time in Nîmes, I remember, the bull galloped halfway round the arena with the banderilla sticking between its eyes; it slapped against the muzzle. The bull thrust its head forward, vomited blood, and the light went out in the open eyes, the black hide turned dusty, the forelegs buckled: it hung dead in the noon air.

Here's where Lynn and Dick live. (They were there. She cried.) And those people whose name I never could remember—whose party William and I went to—where that man forgot his wife and had to go back upstairs . . .

Hundred-and-tenth. That burned-out body shop's been here as long as I remember, next to the fly-bitten luncheonette called HARR 'S PARAD/E. I forget the name of the bridge we're crossing. I always liked bridges.

Here the houses are more alien than Harlem. Who builds these neat homes on highways next to secondhand car lots with neon green and yellow pennants clapping in the wind? Motel Row. A Carvel's. McDonald's. Limbo. If I can find a single fine proportion or one graceful line, I shall be saved!

The cemetery wall goes on and goes on.

In Rome, I insisted on mistaking our direction, and Zeus and I walked all the way round the outside of Vatican City. For an hour and a half I kept thinking any moment we would come in sight of the right arm of St. Peter's colonnade. There's a cobbled path, a high, blank wall; on the right, nothing but weeds. At midday we met an angel, disguised as an ancient gardener, on his knees scraping the moss off cobble after cobble. He said it was his job to keep them tidy, but I believe it is to measure eternity on earth.

Inside the cemetery gates the driver gets a ticket with my number on it, and we move at a round pace between the graves, double back up the next row, down a third. "I had not thought death had undone so many." (The last line is banal even though it's in French, yet it's true too. Your heart, sisters, will ache like mine to be dead.) Graves to the right, graves to the left of me. We're massed on this hill. Imagine an army of us pitched against all of you . . .

They've stopped the first limousine around the bend. Reform funeral directors know that one can barely suffer the coffin at rest, much less when it is being moved, which suggests the motionless contents: me. It musn't be seen like this, suspended on two poles over a hole in the ground. They hide me under two pieces of faded canvas.

The mourners are coming up the hill. The sky is a wild blue. Is that William crying?

"Say after me, '*Sh'ma Yisroel . . .*' and throw on a handful of earth."

Is that all? The mourners are turning to descend. Already men with shovels are piling on the dirt.

Hold it a moment! Wait! If you wait, I'll tell you a story. I got the idea flying low over a mountain that looked like Gulliver face down, straining to rise although a million Lilliputian threads have him pegged to the ground. I imagined Lazarus tugged equally by Christ's power to raise him and his yearning to stay under. I never wrote the story because I couldn't figure where to go from there. Stop! Not yet! I'll tell you another one. There's a young man, in a subway accident. He's not actually hurting—probably in shock. He's watching the firemen put out the fires and coughs from the smoke. A policeman with a clipboard is taking down his name, address, place and date of birth, name of his father, his mother's maiden name. The doctor arrives and gives him an injection. They bring blankets from somewhere. He's pronounced dead and the subway resumes its journey. It stops at the regular Seventh Avenue IRT local stations, One-hundred-third, -tenth, One-hundred-sixteenth, and out into the sunlight at One hundred and twenty-fifth Street and back underground. The next stop begins to look unfamiliar, though he must have been here one time or another. It's the turnstiles' not being where he would expect them. At the next station the wastebaskets puzzle him, because they aren't orange, and the tiles on the walls have a wrong, a foreign, look like the Métro, but now it's the material that's alien. And there are inexplicable free-standing objects . . . I never wrote this story either. I don't write science fiction.

How do you describe things whose raison d'etre is that they are out of ken? Meanwhile, Jimmy travels on through the *ur*-particles of chaos—a sort of homogenized matter—out into Nothing, which cannot be written, which was the point of the story.

The thud of earth falling is duller now. More layers cover me. They say that ghosts come back from the grave to get retribution, or to make amends, but have you never left a lover and felt your bowels rip, and didn't you go back just once more and just once more? Let me haunt, if it's only for a little while! I'll get used to the separation bit by bit.

Ulla and Maurie drive William home.

The key in the lock echoes. "I'm sorry about all the clothes all over the floor," says William. "Lucinella was going to find a chest of drawers . . . "

Ulla says she'll make the coffee. "You sit, William."

"I'm okay," says William.

"I'll get the door," Maurie says.

It's Winterneet. He takes William's hand and says, "Just the other day, in Times Square, I was standing as close to her as I am to you now . . . "

Ulla says, "I'll get the door."

Betterwheatling and Cilena, and Meyers. Meyers says, "I've brought a goddamn apple pie."

"I know," Ulla says, "I keep making coffee. Let me go find a plate. Sit down, William."

"I'm fine," William says. "You'll have to sit on the floor, I'm sorry. Lucinella was always going to get chairs but never found one that was elegant and honest, both."

Maurie says, "William should go to Yaddo for a week or two. Shall I give them a call?"

William says thank you, but no, he's got to clean up here.

The doorbell rings and George and Mary Friend arrive,

and Pavlovenka, and Frank and Alice Friendling. Bert has come all the way in from New Jersey; Benjamin, Newman, they all come. Ulla brings them coffee. “Thank you,” they say. “No, no pie, thank you.” Nobody feels like eating. (Later they’ll get hungry.)

Meyers says he got it at the place down in the Village. Betterwheatling says he know a better place way over on First Avenue, he thinks it’s in the Fifties, where thy bake their own.

They’ve stopped talking about me.

William says, “Lucinella’s favorite food used to be bread and butter.” He gets up, walks out the door into the hall, gets on the elevator, and rides up and down, holding his finger on the CLOSE button. Then he goes back to his friends. They’re sitting quietly, talking.

Betterwheatling is saying he saw a woman climbing the subway stairs one step at a time. Her right shoe was unlaced and she had no sock on, so you could see the foot was covered with sores. Betterwheatling says he had some notion of giving her his sock or some other sock, which seemed implausible, so he decided it could not hurt as badly as it looked and ran past, up the stairs, and downstairs to the local platform, and took out his paperback. When he looked up, the woman was still putting her right foot one step up and bringing the left behind it. His train came. Before they closed the doors, Betterwheatling says, he looked up and saw the woman putting her right foot down the first step of the local stairs.

Alice Friendling says once she saw a blind man carrying what looked like a box of tools, and she remembers thinking: The man is in his fifties and has managed all this time without *me*, he probably knows there are stairs in front of him. But he blind man fell headlong down the stairs. She says the toolbox made an awful clatter. The light in the room is gone. Nobody moves.

Meyers says his mother died about the time he won his Pulitzer. He says he asked her, "Mother, are you proud of what I've done?" She answered, "What do I care what you're doing. I'm dying."

Someone goes to make drinks.

Meyers says, "I always meant to put it in a poem."

"Will you send it to *The Magazine?*" asks Maurie.

"I sent you five poems a week ago," says William. "You didn't so much as acknowledge receipt."

Maurie says, "I don't have a secretary. I've been away. I've had the flu. And now with Lucinella dying . . . "

"Poor old Lucinella! So embarrassing!" says Betterwheatling.

Winterneet glares. "How do you mean, 'embarrassing'?"

"Winterneet, come off it," I say. "You know what Betterwheatling means. I saw you at my funeral trying not to smile." But I have no voice with which to argue. "He means I've slipped on the Great Banana Peel and am permanently floored!" I shout.

"I mean," says Betterwheatling, "how would *you* like everybody standing there, knowing that you're dead?"

Betterwheatling's saying what I mean turns me on and I reach out to touch him. I remember at a party once, Friendling, whom I'd known for years but never really talked to, said something—I forget what it was that moved me. I saw him look down, surprised to see it was my hand on his elbow, and yet I didn't want a thing, I swear, except to feel his male and human arm bending inside the cloth tube of his sleeve.

Betterwheatling does not look down. Nothing has touched him. I yank at his arm, pound it. I hurl myself at Betterwheatling. Screeching, I grab the damn pie plate to send it crashing and cause some echo in this world, but they go on, quietly, talking. Dear god, if ghosts had the capacity to polter it wouldn't be for mischief but from a longing to connect with matter, if it's only to move it from here to there. But I have no forefinger and thumb with which to take hold of anything.

When you come to think about it, doesn't incorporeality *mean* that I neither displace air nor rival any other object in it and can affect no thing. We have maligned the incubus! I think it comes into our beds without equipment, in a desperation of tenderness.

I have no cheek to lay against William's back. He has doubled over.

Maurie says, "I'm going to call Yaddo," and William says, "Yes, please. And then would you please go home. Lucinella was more fun than anybody. Also, she could be so awful I still want to murder her. What do I do now with all that unfinished business? *Please,* Ulla, don't start tidying, it's something for me to do when you've gone. No, really, I don't need, I don't *want*, anyone sleeping over." He says, "Come back tomorrow, but now, please, all of you, go home." He is embraced, embraces, closes the door behind them, and leans his head against it, devastated at their going.

William picks up a cup and saucer and puts it down again. Poor William, you always thought that you helped tidy because you held two glasses and walked behind me, talking about who'd been here and what they'd said or meant. We agreed it was the best part of every party, but why did I have to talk *and* tidy? Why did I mind? William goes into the bathroom and douses his face with water. I used to think, William, that it wasn't love if you left your towel scrumpled after use, though I told and told you it couldn't dry. I was always *going* to love you, William, as soon as you shaped up. That's why I nagged and nagged you to straighten your towel out. Also, you do have a tendency to whine if somebody turns down a poem, and the back of your neck is skimpy. I used to kiss it to apologize, or was that love?

William has picked up my shoes and two pairs of panties from the floor—poor William, the ghoulish job of getting rid of my bits and pieces. He puts them down again and lies back on the couch, though he knows that bedspread costs four bucks to dry-clean, but now I *know* he will put his dirty shoes on white wool through eternity, I don't mind. Dear William, hope was the enemy! There's not a man alive, now, I couldn't love, William, now I'd know how!

Yesterday William arrived at Yaddo and when he saw the lilac in full bloom he wept, but this morning it is even more purple. Once I saw a dancer gain the top of his leap, leap higher, and stand in the air.

It is after noon. This is the third time William comes out of his study and goes around the back. Daily he takes in meat and drink, uses part, and gives the rest back. His elbow bends his arm at an efficient angle so that his thumb and forefinger can close on the tab of his zipper. Who says life isn't sweet with the sun still high for hours to come?

Through his study window William watches J. D. Winterneet walk up the drive with an old man's careful step. William opens his mouth and howls and looks around shocked to be making such a noise. There's no one to hear him, except me.

At the table the silver bowl is full of lilacs. Since ghosts have neither breath nor noses, I can smell nothing, but then I never was very live to odors. William's poems are full of fragrances. He leans into the heavy sweetness, and because the conversation is friendly and funny, William aches for me, knows now that I really am dead, deader than I was a week ago; daily I recede and William hauls me into the dining room by saying "Lucinella always said . . ." But even Winterneet, who used rather to like me, cannot, on such short notice, come up with the appropriate feeling to entertain a dead woman over his chocolate mousse and whipped cream, and it does *me* no good, William! The time has come to argue myself to my conclusion. Ergo, if I have not the wherewithals to speak, or touch, or smell, I know I have no ears either. The world's sound has switched off. As on a silent television screen I see William's head laid back. Only the convulsive motion of his shoulders tells me he laughs. I told you I'd go in a little while. Sense by sense I unthink myself. I think I'm ready now to know I see nothing. Where is William? Where's everybody! I can no longer see William laughing, nor Winterneet raise his cup of coffee to his lips, one elbow on the massive table with its carved and foolish legs. I no longer see the silver bowl full of flowers, nor feel my grief at my absence nor know anything for in the end there is no word

TITLES IN THE COMPANION SERIES

THE ART OF THE NOVELLA

BARTLEBY THE SCRIVENER / HERMAN MELVILLE
THE LESSON OF THE MASTER / HENRY JAMES
MY LIFE / ANTON CHEKHOV
THE DEVIL / LEO TOLSTOY
THE TOUCHSTONE / EDITH WHARTON
THE HOUND OF THE BASKERVILLES / ARTHUR CONAN DOYLE
THE DEAD / JAMES JOYCE
FIRST LOVE / IVAN TURGENEV
A SIMPLE HEART / GUSTAVE FLAUBERT
THE MAN WHO WOULD BE KING / RUDYARD KIPLING
MICHAEL KOHLHAAS / HEINRICH VON KLEIST
THE BEACH OF FALESÁ / ROBERT LOUIS STEVENSON
THE HORLA / GUY DE MAUPASSANT
THE ETERNAL HUSBAND / FYODOR DOSTOEVSKY
THE MAN THAT CORRUPTED HADLEYBURG / MARK TWAIN
THE LIFTED VEIL / GEORGE ELIOT
THE GIRL WITH THE GOLDEN EYES / HONORÉ DE BALZAC
A SLEEP AND A FORGETTING / WILLIAM DEAN HOWELLS
BENITO CERENO / HERMAN MELVILLE
MATHILDA / MARY SHELLEY
STEMPENYU: A JEWISH ROMANCE / SHOLEM ALEICHEM
FREYA OF THE SEVEN ISLES / JOSEPH CONRAD
HOW THE TWO IVANS QUARRELLED / NIKOLAI GOGOL
MAY DAY / F. SCOTT FITZGERALD
RASSELAS, PRINCE ABYSSINIA / SAMUEL JOHNSON
THE DECEITFUL MARRIAGE / MIGUEL DE CERVANTES
THE LEMOINE AFFAIR / MARCEL PROUST
THE COXON FUND / HENRY JAMES
THE DEATH OF IVAN ILYICH / LEO TOLSTOY
TALES OF BELKIN / ALEXANDER PUSHKIN

THE CONTEMPORARY ART OF THE NOVELLA

OTHER TITLES IN

THE CONTEMPORARY ART OF THE NOVELLA SERIES

THE PATHSEEKER / IMRE KERTÉSZ

THE DEATH OF THE AUTHOR / GILBERT ADAIR

THE NORTH OF GOD / STEVE STERN

CUSTOMER SERVICE / BENOÎT DUTEURTRE

BONSAI / ALEJANDRO ZAMBRA

ILLUSION OF RETURN / SAMIR EL-YOUSSEF

CLOSE TO JEDENEW / KEVIN VENNEMANN

A HAPPY MAN / HANSJÖRG SCHERTENLEIB

SHOPLIFTING FROM AMERICAN APPAREL / TAO LIN

LUCINELLA / LORE SEGAL

SANDOKAN / NANNI BALESTRINI